"Any man y something s

Jessica swallowed

"Marry." Keir enunciated it very clearly.

"Oh, no. I may have said some things about the right wife being an important consideration in the corporate world, but I hardly think that applies to you."

"Why, what's the problem?"

"Oh, nothing much. It's just that I have absolutely no desire to marry you, Keir."

"Who said anything about actually getting married?"

"You did. Unless you mean this would be just an act till you get your deal nailed down?"

Leigh Michaels has always loved happy endings. Even when she was a child, if a book's conclusion didn't please her, she'd make up her own. And, though she always wanted to write fiction, she very sensibly planned to earn her living as a newspaper reporter. That career didn't work out, however, and she found herself writing for Harlequin Mills & Boon instead—in the kind of happy ending only a romance novelist could dream up!

Leigh likes to hear from readers; you can write to her at PO Box 935, Ottumwa, Iowa, 52501-0935 USA.

Recent titles by the same author:

TAMING A TYCOON
TIES THAT BLIND
THE ONLY MAN FOR MAGGIE

MARRYING
THE BOSS!

BY
LEIGH MICHAELS

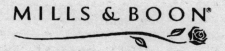

MILLS & BOON®

MILLS & BOON and MILLS & BOON with the Rose Device
are registered trademarks of the publisher.

First published in Great Britain 1997
Harlequin Mills & Boon Limited,
Eton House, 18-24 Paradise Road, Richmond, Surrey, TW9 1SR

© Leigh Michaels 1996

ISBN 0 263 80034 2

Set in Times Roman 10 on 12 pt
02-9703-55320 C

Printed and bound in Great Britain
by Mackays of Chatham PLC, Chatham

CHAPTER ONE

SHE checked the math three times, but it still came out the same. Of course it was nothing new to find the balance in the bank account pitifully small after all the bills were paid. In the six months since Jessica Bennington had started to work as office manager of Toolshop Software, cash flow problems had been a regular occurrence. This time, however, was different. She hadn't written all the checks yet, but the money was already gone. Frankly, she didn't see how they were going to scrape by.

She put the check register in the drawer and started to flip through the mail. It wasn't as if the company carried a great deal of overhead, after all, and even a few customer orders would help to ease the money crunch for another week or two.

The red light on the telephone was still blinking, she realized. She wondered if Keir had picked it up and then put the caller on hold once more, or if he'd ignored the intercom buzzer altogether. She shook her head at the phone and pushed her chair back.

It was only a couple of steps from her work area to the door of what could euphemistically be called the inner office. Privately, Jessica thought of it as the bear's den—though she suspected sometimes that a real bear might keep his cave neater than her boss kept his office.

She tapped on the door, didn't get an answer and went in.

The room was hardly more than pocket-size, and the walls seemed to bulge in order to contain all the equipment inside. There were two state-of-the-art computers, linked by a twisted maze of cables to each other and to a massive old printer. The sleek, expensive computers contrasted oddly with the makeshift workstations they sat on—scarred pieces of plywood balanced across badly battered Army green filing cabinets. In a corner, half-hidden under a stack of books, was a gray plastic box housing one of the earliest personal computers ever made.

Manuals, sketches, long banners of tractor-feed paper and catalogs had spilled off the rumpled couch and were scattered across the carpet. Jessica couldn't see the phone, but she spotted the cord. It snaked through the pile of papers and disappeared under the edge of the couch.

In the room's only chair, pulled up in front of one of the rickety workstations, sat her boss. Obviously unaware of her presence, Keir Saunders was leaning forward with a frown, eyes intent on the computer screen as hundreds of lines of programming code scrolled upward at a pace Jessica found blinding.

She stood in the doorway for a moment, reluctant to interrupt, waiting for him to notice her. He looked tired, she thought. His shoulders were slumped as if he'd been sitting there far too long, his jeans were rumpled, and his curly dark brown hair was askew, as if he'd been running his fingers through it. But then, she thought, Keir's hair looked that way most of the time.

"Keir," she said. "You have a phone call, remember?"

He didn't take his eyes off the screen. "Hasn't he given up yet?"

"No. And since it's that real estate guy, and he insists on talking to you about the software you promised him by last week, you'd better hope he doesn't hang up."

Keir sighed, pushed a button to stop the scrolling commands and leaned back in his chair. "I'm debugging a program, Jess."

He was the only person on earth who had ever called her Jess. Jessica had long since given up on making him understand that she preferred her full name.

"I've been fighting this thing since late last night," he went on, "and I've almost got it. Another couple of hours—"

There were lines of exhaustion in his face, Jessica noted with a trace of sympathy, and across his chin lay the dark shadow of stubble. "Is it his program you're working on?"

Keir shook his head. "Oh, no—it's far more interesting than tracking real estate prices."

"Which I suppose means there's no profit in it?" Jessica unearthed the telephone and set it squarely in front of him. "Well, take a break from the bugs and rest your eyes. And while you're doing that, you may as well talk nicely to this guy and see if you can soothe him down so we can keep his business."

He put a hand on the telephone, but he didn't pick it up. "I suppose that means we have cash flow problems again."

"What do you mean, *again*?" Jessica asked dryly.

"That bad, huh? Well, you'll figure it out. You always have before."

"I'm glad you have so much faith in me, Keir, but—"

"Oh, I do, Jess." He sounded perfectly earnest. "You've worked magic around here. It was the luckiest day of my life when you came in to apply for this job. I haven't had to worry about a thing since."

Before Jessica could give the snort she felt like indulging herself in, he'd leaned forward again to stare at the screen. "Wait a second—there it is!" He turned a brilliant sapphire gaze on Jessica. "The bug. After I've been looking for it all these hours, it's right there on the screen where you made me stop it when you came in. Jess, you're my lucky charm. My mascot. My amulet—"

Jessica didn't believe a word of it. The moment she walked out the door, he'd once more forget she existed. "I'm also your conscience," she interrupted. "Answer the call, Keir. I'm going out to get a sandwich—want me to bring your usual?"

He nodded and picked up the receiver. "Hello, Vaughn," he said, and a moment later he stretched a long arm out to the stack of papers that had slid off the couch. He snagged one sheet from the pile and said, "I've got it right here. It will be a bit of a challenge, but I think you'll be happier if we take the extra time and add fuzzy logic to the program. We'll just modify the parameters of the field to allow for date ranges instead of precise entries. And—"

Jessica shook her head. The thing that really amazed her about all the clutter was that Keir never appeared to lose anything. Sometimes he didn't even seem to look at a pile of paper as he reached into it and pulled out the single page he needed. As for whatever he was talking about, the whole thing was beyond her comprehension. *Fuzzy logic?* Wasn't that a contradiction in terms? And what could it possibly have to do with real estate?

It was a good thing, she reflected as she got her coat from the rack and faced the sharp October breeze, that her job required only that she understand the common-sense basics of office management, not computers themselves—or the geniuses who programmed them.

Though there *was* one thing the erratic Keir Saunders was good for, Jessica thought. The overwhelming contrast between him and Trevor McIntyre certainly made a woman appreciate a good thing when she saw it. After spending her days with Keir, it was pure joy to date Trevor, to be treasured and taken care of, indulged and appreciated as a woman instead of just a handy piece of office equipment.

She shivered in the chilly breeze as she crossed the street to the deli. If this wind kept up, the last of autumn's gorgeous leaves would soon be gone, whipped from the trees. There was already a hint of frost in the air, and the sky was gray and heavy as if snow was just around the corner. It looked as if Kansas City was in for a long winter.

She stepped up to the deli counter. "A hot pastrami on rye with sharp Cheddar, and a bologna on white with mayo," she told the clerk.

The woman reached for the bread and slapped on the fillings with the efficient ease of long practice. "Did your boss work all night again?" she asked idly.

Jessica nodded.

"I thought so. He came in just at closing time for a peanut-butter-with-jelly-and-banana sandwich to go, and he only orders those when he's on some kind of a deadline."

Jessica shuddered. "I thought his usual bologna was bad enough, but peanut butter and—" Words failed her.

The clerk cut the sandwiches with two quick blows of the knife and reached for waxed paper to wrap them. "How'd a classy lady like you manage to end up working for a guy like him, anyway?"

Jessica's mouth tightened. It was only a casual question, she was sure, but the query annoyed her nevertheless—mostly, she supposed, because of her sensitivity. A job as the office manager of a tiny, struggling computer software company certainly hadn't been what she'd foreseen for herself back in her finishing school days. If she'd had any idea what lay in her future, she'd have made darned sure her education had prepared her for something more than making charming conversation and arranging charity bazaars. Of course, all those bazaars had lent her the organizational skills she was putting to such good use now.

Or, at least, *trying* to put to use, she corrected herself. Organizing Keir Saunders was something like trying to harness a hailstorm.

The clerk was looking at her oddly. ''Did I say something to offend you? I don't mean there's anything wrong with him, exactly. He'd even be reasonably good-looking if he'd get his hair cut and shave on a regular schedule and wear something besides jeans and that awful, ratty gray sweater. I only meant it's obvious from the way you dress that you don't belong in that dinky little office.''

''Thanks,'' Jessica said equably. It was nice to know that someone appreciated the designer cut of her pine-green suit. It had been the last gift her grandmother gave her, and though it was more than a year old now, the classic lines were as stylish as ever. Which was a good thing, Jessica told herself, since with the way the bank balance looked at Toolshop Software, it would be a long time before she could hope for any sort of raise. Her current salary certainly didn't allow her to dress in the style that Clementine Bennington had thought appropriate for her only granddaughter.

As she waited for traffic to clear so she could cross the street once more, Jessica surveyed the narrow frontage of the building that housed Toolshop Software. The most run-down and dilapidated on a block where every structure had seen better days, it was also the smallest. That fact was what had given Keir Saunders's business its name, he'd told her on the day he'd hired her.

''All the best computer companies seem to have started off in somebody's garage,'' he'd said. ''Since I didn't have a garage handy, I had to settle for something more the size of a woodshed—but I hope to move up to a garage one day.'' His eyes had sparkled as he said it, and his grin held not a hint of self-consciousness or embarrassment.

''I should have known right then that this wasn't exactly a Fortune 500 company just waiting to be discovered,'' Jessica muttered. But with her lack of experience and training, jobs hadn't been so plentiful that she could be choosy.

Keir was still on the phone, leaning back in his chair and waving his hands as if the client could see his gestures. He talked a lot with his hands, she'd noticed. Jessica wondered if he realized they were probably his best feature—long-fingered, strong, beautifully shaped.

She quietly set his sandwich and a can of Coke beside the keyboard and went to her desk. She picked at her pastrami while she tried once more to make the bank balance stretch to cover the outstanding bills. Electricity, rent on the building, telephone charges, the astronomical fees Keir ran up every month on the computer networks... With winter coming on, she'd no doubt have to budget for some sort of fuel, as well. She made a mental note to ask Keir about that right away. The building felt chilly today.

The phone rang, and she answered it absently, still scanning the unpaid bills.

''Jessica?''

The sound of Trevor McIntyre's voice sent a glow through Jessica's entire body. He seldom called her at work, and of course Jessica didn't expect him to. Trevor was a mid-level manager at one of Kansas City's largest corporations, a young man on his way up the ladder—and far too busy to take time out of his workday for personal matters.

Almost automatically, she lowered her voice to the soft, husky timbre he'd told her he admired so much. "Hello, Trevor."

"What's going on over there? I've been trying to get through for an hour."

"I'm sorry about that. Keir's had the phone tied up."

"That figures—I suppose he can't afford two phone lines."

Jessica almost pointed out that Toolshop *did* have two lines—though she supposed the fact that the second one was dedicated to the computers made it a moot point. And she couldn't exactly blame Trevor for being annoyed. His time was too valuable to waste an hour of it on trying to make a single phone call.

"Well, it *was* business," she said mildly. "What's going on? Is something wrong?"

"No. Oh, no. I just wondered if we could have dinner tonight."

"On a Tuesday? I thought you always played racquetball on Tuesdays."

Was there just an instant's hesitation before Trevor answered?

"My partner's away on a business trip," he said. "Anyway, I need to see you."

He seemed almost diffident, Jessica thought. He'd never sounded quite so urgent before—and he seldom asked to see her in the middle of the week, either. Though they'd been dating for nearly a year, they'd never discussed anything much further away than the next weekend. They'd certainly never talked about a future together, though Jessica had to admit she'd had her hopes for some time now. Did this hesitation of his mean—*could* it mean—that he was growing truly serious about her, too?

"It'll have to be early, I'm afraid," Trevor went on. "I've committed myself to making an appearance later in the evening at the company president's house."

She wondered if that was an invitation of sorts. He'd never taken her to any of Union Manufacturing's functions before.

"Can I pick you up at the office about six?"

"Of course," she said, her throat so tight with hope and wonder that she could hardly speak, and put the telephone down.

She had to take several deep breaths before she could stop her head from spinning and settle down to her work, and even then, she had trouble concentrating.

The teenager who came in after school each day to handle the packing and shipping duties noticed. "You look like there's a light inside you," he said.

Jessica smiled. "Thanks, Randy. That's very poetic." She pushed a few envelopes across her desk to him. "There's not much work for you today, I'm afraid."

"Oh, that's all right. After I've got these programs copied and ready to go, I'll just polish up some of my own code. What happened to you, anyway? Must have been wonderful to make you shine like that." He looked at her almost slyly. "Is it something to do with Keir?"

Jessica blinked in surprise. What could he possibly imagine happening to Keir that would make her glow? Unless he thought there was something *romantic* between them . . . No, that was too incredible a scenario for even a boy like Randy to dream up—despite the fact that he seemed to be thinking about girls any time he wasn't actually working a computer.

Randy grinned. "Don't worry, I won't say anything about it to him."

"Good," Jessica said dryly. She didn't bother to deny Randy's suspicions. Doing so would probably only make him wonder more.

He fired up the old computer that stood on a side table and started making copies of some of Keir's software programs.

Jessica went back to the bills. Perhaps some kind of a direct-mail advertising campaign would pay off, she thought. If they could get a good mailing list of people who used products similar to theirs, without spending a fortune on it...

She and Randy were both still hard at work when the door opened and three men in dark business suits, blindingly white shirts and identical dark red ties came in.

Randy looked up in wide-eyed wonder. Jessica dropped her pencil.

The office was small and the men were big—not fat, but tall and broad and bulky. Without a word, they surveyed every square inch of the room, and Jessica could almost read the disapproval in the cool appraisal.

She had no trouble understanding that reaction. She'd felt much the same way on the day the employment agency had sent her to see Keir Saunders, when she'd first walked into this room. It was better now—the dust was gone, and she'd managed to bring some order to the mess. But Toolshop was still obviously a shoestring operation.

Her desk, for instance, was an unvarnished wooden door balanced across two filing cabinets only slightly less banged-up than the ones in Keir's office. When Keir had arrived at work one morning carrying the door, balancing it easily despite its weight, and announced what it was for, Jessica had looked at him askance and pointed out that there was a hole in one side.

"Of course there is," he'd said. "How do you think I managed to get it free? A carpenter mismeasured and cut the opening for the knob in the wrong spot. Look at it as an advantage." He'd grabbed a plastic bag, stuck it through the hole, taped down the edges and said, "Now you have a built-in wastebasket."

The three men did not look any more impressed than Jessica had been.

She stood up. "May I help you?"

The cool appraisal of three sets of eyes focused on her. One of the men said, "We're looking for Toolshop Software, but—"

She smiled. "You've found it."

"Keir Saunders's outfit?"

"Yes. May I tell him who's here?"

"He probably won't recognize the names. Just tell him he won't regret taking the time to see us." He held out a business card.

That, Jessica thought, could almost sound like a threat. From the look on his face, Randy agreed—his eyes had grown as big as saucers, and he'd flinched when the man reached into his breast pocket, as if he was expecting to see a gun.

"Have a seat, gentlemen." Too late, she remembered that there were only two chairs for visitors, both of them the folding variety and both a bit rickety. "Randy, if you'll give up your chair to one of these gentlemen—"

He leaped up. "I should be going," he said. "I didn't realize what time—"

"Stick around till I come back, Randy." It was clearly an order not to leave these unknown clients alone, and Randy wilted.

The men were still standing when Jessica eased through the door into Keir's office.

Except for the half-eaten sandwich, which lay beside the keyboard, the scene might as well have been a time warp from that morning. Code was scrolling across the computer screen, and Keir was staring intently at it.

"I thought you said you found the bug," Jessica said.

He nodded but didn't look up. "One of them. A big one, too. But now there's something else locking up the program."

"Oh. There are three guys to see you."

That got his attention. "What kind of guys?"

"Black suits, white shirts, red ties."

"Suits? Doesn't sound like my kind of people."

"Randy obviously thinks they're Mafia," Jessica said. "But one of them gave me his card, so I'd say he's legitimate."

Keir took the card between two fingers. "I never heard of him. Or the company, either."

"Well, maybe they're bankruptcy attorneys. At the rate we're going—"

"Is it that bad, Jess?"

"The way things look at the moment, by the time I write Randy a check for today's work, there won't be anything left for you to pay the rent on your apartment or buy food."

"Oh, I've given that up," Keir said easily.

"What? Eating?"

"No. The apartment. I was spending all my time here anyway, so I thought it was pointless to waste the money on another place. There's a couch here, and a shower— what else does anybody need?"

Jessica wasn't even surprised. It was amazing what a few months of working for this man could do to a woman's mind, she thought. "Well, a furnace might be a nice addition," she pointed out. "I turned the thermostat up an hour ago, but there doesn't seem to be any heat coming through the registers."

"Oh, the heating system gets a little balky sometimes. You might want to bring a sweater."

Jessica didn't like the airy note in his voice. "Speaking of sweaters, don't you think you should take yours off before you greet these guys?"

"Why? You said yourself it's cold in here."

"The woman at the deli called it ratty—and I think she was giving you a compliment. Don't you want to make a good impression? Isn't there a sports jacket around somewhere?"

Keir glanced around vaguely as if half-expecting one to materialize before him.

Jessica finally found the jacket under a pile of computer manuals. Luckily it was corduroy, and a vigorous shake eliminated many of the wrinkles.

Keir sighed, stripped off his sweater and put the jacket on. "All right," he said. "Send the suits in."

Jessica glanced at her watch. "I suppose you want me to stay in case you need something?" she asked reluctantly. "I've got a date tonight, but—"

"With the rising executive, no doubt? Oh, run along— I wouldn't want to put a kink in his schedule by keeping you late. Besides," Keir said, squaring his shoulders and turning toward the door, "if Randy's right and the suits *do* turn out to be the Mafia, this way maybe you'll live to tell the tale."

He was kidding, Jessica thought. At least, she hoped so.

The wind had picked up as the sun sank, and Jessica shivered as she crossed the sidewalk to where Trevor had double-parked his sports car. He was fiddling with the controls when she got in, and she leaned back in the soft leather seat and luxuriated in the stream of warmth that surrounded her. "Sorry I'm a bit late—Keir had some last-minute visitors." She wiggled her toes. "The heat feels awfully good."

"That's odd. I was thinking it was chilly, and trying to figure out which bit of equipment wasn't working right. I guess I'll have to take it back to the dealer again."

"Well, it feels wonderful compared to where I've been." Jessica regretted the words the moment they were out, for Trevor would probably make another comment about what Toolshop couldn't seem to afford.

But he didn't. He pulled the car into traffic and said, "Is Felicity's all right with you?"

"Of course. The food's always wonderful." It was also Jessica's favorite restaurant, and the quietest one she knew—with widely spaced tables that allowed private conversations, and nooks and crannies that made interruptions by other diners less likely. And it was also where Trevor had taken her for dinner on their very first date....

Jessica's heart beat just a little faster. She'd never thought of Trevor as the sentimental sort, but there *was* something different about him tonight; it wasn't her imagination. He kept stealing little glances at her and running his hand over his sleek blond hair as if he was nervous.

For the first time she allowed herself to imagine him proposing. It was oddly endearing, to think of the self-assured Trevor hesitating, perhaps even stammering over the most important question of his life. And what about her answer? It would be *yes,* of course, but exactly how should she say it? It would be silly to repeat the Victorian cliché about it all being too sudden, but she didn't want to seem overeager, either....

Trevor flicked on the turn signal and pulled onto a main thoroughfare. "You mean he actually does some business now and then?"

Jessica was startled by the sudden comment, and it took a moment to pull herself back from her thoughts. "You mean Keir?"

"This is the first time you've ever mentioned him having clients in the office."

She almost said she wasn't so sure they were clients, but that would only lead to more questions. "A lot of our business is mail order, you know. Keir writes a piece of software, puts a basic version of it out on the computer networks so people can try it out, and if they like it they send an order for the full version."

"And he makes money that way."

It wasn't a question, so Jessica didn't answer it.

"Well, at least he's got sense enough to limit his contact with the public," Trevor said. "With his lack of polish, he wouldn't stand a ghost of a chance in the corporate world. There are rules in business—standards that have to be met. Can you imagine that ape entertaining the big boss at a dinner party?"

Jessica could, as a matter of fact. The menu would probably include bologna sandwiches and soft drinks straight from the can.

It was still so early that Felicity's wasn't busy. But then the restaurant never looked crowded, even when there were people standing in line waiting for their tables.

Jessica left her coat in the cloakroom and brushed a hand across her wool skirt. The suit was the most flattering thing she owned. How glad she was that she'd pulled it out of the closet this morning!

The maître d' greeted Trevor soberly and said hello to Jessica with a smile and a tiny bow. "It's a pleasure to see you again, Miss Bennington. How nice you look tonight."

She was absurdly pleased at the compliment. "Thank you, Jonathan."

He showed them to a table in a corner even more out-of-the-way than usual. She couldn't help wondering if Trevor had requested that particularly private nook. If, indeed, he intended to propose . . .

Don't let yourself get carried away, Jessica warned herself, and very deliberately she turned her mind to enjoying the evening. Places like Felicity's were nothing

new to her, but she relished them much more now that
an evening out was an occasion and a steak a rare treat.

"He treats you like an old friend," Trevor grumbled.

"Well, I came here with my grandmother for years."

"A phony friend, at that. Telling you how nice you
look in that old suit—"

Jessica's pleasure in Jonathan's compliment evapo-
rated. How silly could she be? No doubt he told every
regular customer that!

"Not that you don't look nice," Trevor added hastily.
"But I know I've seen you wearing that suit at least a
dozen times, and I imagine he has, too."

Jessica took a deep breath and let it out, as her grandmother had taught her, and smiled. "Sorry if you're
bored by it," she said sweetly. "But there hasn't been a
whole lot of money for designer clothes lately."

"I know. And you mustn't think I blame you for it.
It's too bad, though." His voice trailed off, and he picked
up the wine list and murmured something to the waiter,
then sat back in his chair with a smile that looked almost
determined. "It's a shame your grandmother didn't plan
a little farther ahead, so she didn't leave you penniless."

"She had no idea how bad things were. And if I had
my choice between being broke now or having her scrimp
and do without in her last years so she could leave me
a nest egg, I wouldn't change a thing. I'm far more prepared to take care of myself than she ever was."

"And that's why you're still working at Woodshed
Software, I suppose?"

"The name is *Toolshop*."

Trevor looked startled. "You certainly sound de-
fensive." He tasted the wine and nodded at the waiter,
who filled Jessica's glass.

It was a very nice domestic red, Jessica noticed. Not
the champagne she'd half-expected. "Well, I owe Keir
something. It's hard to get a job these days without ex-

perience—but how do you get experience if no one will hire you? He took a chance on me. I have a perfectly good degree in general studies that prepared me to do absolutely nothing to earn a living. But now that I have an employment record, a few months on the job and a good recommendation from my boss when I decide to move on—''

''I wouldn't care to bet on what his recommendation will be worth. But at least you're not deluded enough to stick around because you think the place is going to make anybody a millionaire. Or has he convinced you to accept stock options instead of a salary?'' Trevor answered his own question. ''No—somebody like Saunders wouldn't have thought of that. Are you ready to order?'' He picked up his menu.

Jessica ordered a small steak and sat back to enjoy her wine. At the next table, she noted, was a man in a dark business suit, his build and red tie reminiscent of the trio who had come to Toolshop this afternoon. There was no other resemblance, but once reminded of the three men, she couldn't help but wonder what that meeting had been about.

With luck, perhaps they would commission Keir to design a new software package—something elaborate and specific to their business, big enough to keep Toolshop in the black for a few months. She couldn't remember the company name on the card, but it had sounded vaguely technical—something to do with engineering, perhaps.

She shouldn't count on anything, she warned herself. Even if that *was* what they wanted, they hadn't looked impressed—and Trevor was right on the money there. Impressions did count, and people were more likely to do business with others who understood the rules. She sighed.

Trevor was looking at his watch. "I hope the kitchen doesn't take long. This damned appointment with the president . . ."

"Perhaps you should tell me what to expect," Jessica suggested.

Trevor looked surprised. "Oh, it's not a party, just a business conference. I'll take you home after dinner. But I really need to talk to you, so I hope the food comes quickly."

There was an odd feeling in the pit of Jessica's stomach. "Is there some reason we can't talk while we're waiting? I'm sure I'll enjoy my meal more if I know what's going on."

He swirled the wine in his glass and said, "Well, I'd planned to discuss it over dessert . . . But I suppose now's as good a time as any. You remember what I was saying before, Jessica, about the rules in business, and the standards that have to be met?"

"Of course."

"And you understand, of course, how things that seem very small can make a big difference in a career. Things like the way a man dresses giving the illusion of success, and making it more likely that he'll ultimately *be* successful."

Jessica nodded.

"And the other choices he makes are even more important. The right wife, for instance."

She swallowed hard.

"When a man doesn't have family connections of his own, it's even more important that he choose a wife who does—who knows how to treat the important people and how to make them comfortable. One who knows how to behave in all those touchy corporate situations, and give a dinner party, and make a perfect home."

In other words, she thought, all the things she herself had been specially trained to do. If he'd tried, he couldn't have constructed a more precise list of the talents Jessica's grandmother had instilled in her. Her heart began to pound.

"Trevor—" Her throat was tight, and the word came out more like a croak.

He frowned. "Please let me finish, Jessica. It's very important that you understand exactly what I'm saying."

There was an unsettled feeling in the pit of her stomach, which puzzled her a little. It wasn't anticipation, she thought. It wasn't even nerves . . .

It was misgiving, she realized with astonishment. The moment she'd been waiting for had come, and she wasn't ready.

This really is too sudden, she thought. *I don't know if I want to spend my life with him.*

She wanted to scream at him to stop, but Trevor went on almost ruthlessly. "But sometimes it's necessary to make sacrifices for the long-term good. A man would be a fool to choose a woman who didn't have the resources that will help him climb the ladder. *All* the resources. That's why I wanted us to talk about this tonight, Jessica."

She was thoroughly confused. "Talk about what?"

"About you. Because as much as I like you, my dear, and as much as I've tried to convince myself that you'd be a suitable wife—"

Jessica was stunned. Of all the smug, self-satisfied, *petty* things to say . . .

"I'm afraid you're lacking in one area that's simply too important to ignore."

All the resources, he'd said. He meant money, of course. The money the Bennington family had once possessed. The money Jessica didn't have now.

"This isn't easy for me, Jessica. But I wanted to tell you myself that my engagement will be announced this weekend." He reached across the table to pat her hand consolingly. "I only wish, of course, that it could have been you."

CHAPTER TWO

LONG training was all that kept Jessica from flinging her glass of wine into Trevor's face and walking out. But Clementine Bennington's lessons had gone too deep. She had brought Jessica up to be too much a lady to create a scene that would humiliate her in a public place—no matter what Trevor deserved.

It was bad enough, she told herself firmly, that he so obviously expected her to be heartbroken over his wedding plans. If she made a fuss about it, she'd only confirm his conviction, and he'd probably preen in delight. But if she kept her head, she could at least save her dignity—and perhaps make the arrogant fool think twice about what he'd done.

She slid her hand out from under his. "How gracious of you to tell me personally." Her voice would have made a glacier sound warm and cuddly.

Trevor shrugged. "I thought it best to warn you so you won't be embarrassed when the public announcement is made."

"Embarrassed? I can't imagine why you thought such happy news might make me uncomfortable."

He looked puzzled. "Well, after all, we have been—"

Jessica cut him off almost in mid-word. "Dating once in a while, that's all. I don't recall that we ever discussed anything further than spending the occasional evening together."

He blinked. "Well, no. We didn't. But since you weren't seeing anyone else, I thought you might expect—"

Jessica's forehead furrowed in mock concern. "Oh, dear—what a problem assumptions can create! I had no idea you intended us to see each other exclusively, so yes, I *have* been seeing other people." It wasn't really a lie, she told herself. She saw lots of people in the course of a day. She hadn't exactly said she was dating any of them, but if he wanted to leap to conclusions...

Trevor was almost sputtering.

"But *of course* you didn't intend that." Jessica let a note of relief creep into her voice. "If you had, you would hardly have been dating your new fiancée at the same time you were seeing me. You *have* been dating her, I assume? You aren't being...forced into this, are you, Trevor?" She sipped her wine. It tasted like vinegar. "But that's none of my business, is it? I do wish you well, and I hope you'll both have all the happiness you deserve."

Trevor looked as if he was about to have apoplexy. Twice, he started to say something and stopped short, obviously realizing the comment would only make him look worse.

Round one to me, Jessica thought. But there was no point in pushing her luck. She couldn't possibly sit through a three-course dinner and continue to smile.

Abruptly, she set her wineglass down, picked up her napkin and began to rub vigorously at her lapel. "Oh, look what I've done," she said. "This is the only good suit I have left, as you so kindly pointed out a few minutes ago. And red wine stains so badly. I'll have to go and put cold water on it immediately." She pushed her chair back to make her escape, not waiting to see if Trevor stood up as she left the table.

The maître d' was at the entrance when Jessica came out of the cloakroom with her coat. "I'm not going back to the table, Jonathan," she murmured. "But do me a favor, will you? Don't tell Mr. McIntyre's waiter—let him think I'll be back any minute."

He didn't turn a hair. "Whatever you wish, Miss Bennington."

It was only a token bit of revenge, but it made Jessica feel a little better. The waiters at Felicity's were trained not to serve any food if one of the guests was temporarily missing. Instead, they held everything up till the guest returned. She wondered how long Trevor would wait for his prime rib before he began to suspect she wasn't coming back at all. With any luck, he might even be late for his appointment.

She smiled at Jonathan, but it took effort. "And since I doubt there will be a tip for either of you from Mr. McIntyre tonight, I'll make it up to you next time I'm in."

He smiled at that. "No need. Serving you is our pleasure." He summoned a cab for her and held the door.

Jessica sank into the welcome dimness of the backseat and closed her eyes. She'd managed to preserve the illusion of calm and serenity. But it had been at terrific cost. Her head felt as if someone had tightened a strap around it, and her fingers were trembling so much she had to clench her hands together.

How dare he treat her that way? And how could she have been such an idiot not to see him clearly all along? Why had that phony charm of his not rung warning bells long before now?

Because you were lonely, she told herself.

With her grandmother so recently gone, Jessica had felt very much alone in the world when she'd met Trevor. Clementine's long illness had been a drain on Jessica, as well, and the shock of finding the small inheritance

she'd expected was nonexistent had been almost a finishing blow.

Only now did she realize that she hadn't ever told
Trevor the whole story. Of course, she hadn't tried to
conceal her circumstances, either—but he must have
picked up hints from their conversations and then
perhaps had her investigated. He must have been almost
as shocked as she had been to find that the Bennington
money was gone.

But even then he'd kept her on the string until he found
somebody better—somebody who met every one of his
requirements. She wondered who the woman was.

When the cab pulled up in front of the brownstone,
Jessica gave her last ten-dollar bill to the cabbie and
walked up the stairs to the third-floor back apartment
where she'd moved shortly after Clementine had died.
She'd done her best to make the small studio into a home,
but it was difficult. Every time she walked in, Jessica
couldn't help but remember her real home, the house
she'd grown up in.

The house had been sold years ago, when Jessica first
went off to boarding school. At the time, she'd been
told that Clementine didn't want the bother of the big
house anymore and preferred the elegant suite she'd
chosen in a nearby retirement complex. It was only much
later, after her grandmother had died, that Jessica
realized the money to pay her school fees and later her
college tuition had come from the sale of the house.

She'd felt guilty about it at first, until she'd realized
that Clementine *had* been happier in the suite, where
help was always available and—with everything
prepaid—she'd never have to concern herself about
money again.

And of course, without the backing of that family
fortune, Jessica couldn't have held onto the house in

any case. But she still thought of it often and with fondness.

The apartment was dark, but she didn't bother to turn the lamps on. The wind had cleared the afternoon's clouds away, letting chilly moonlight pour down from a pitch-black sky over a colorless landscape. She pulled a chair around to the window and stared out.

The starkness of the view suited Jessica's mood precisely. Her initial burst of anger had burned itself out, leaving a dull ache behind her eyes and a dry lump in her throat. She had cared about Trevor. She had built her hopes of a future around him, far more than she had allowed herself to realize—until those hopes came crashing down.

And now she had some serious thinking to do.

Keir's rusty old car was parked behind the building when Jessica got off the bus the next morning. She wondered why she hadn't suspected earlier that he'd simply moved into his office, because no matter how early she'd arrived in the last couple of weeks, he'd already been at his computer.

But she'd thought it was just the new program that was fascinating him. It wasn't the first time she'd seen him work day after day from dawn to exhaustion. Once he'd figured out a solution to a problem that intrigued him, the man seemed driven to get it all down so it couldn't slip away, and then to polish each separate command until it performed flawlessly.

She made a pot of coffee and carried a cup into his office. He seemed absorbed, so she set it beside the computer and stood quietly, watching his long fingers flash over the keyboard.

Keir didn't look up, and his fingers didn't miss a keystroke. "Jess, is there a reason you're standing there as if somebody nailed you to the floor?"

"I need to talk to you, Keir."

"About money? Or is it the real estate software again?"

She moved a stack of papers and sat on the edge of the couch. "That's only part of it."

Keir pushed back his chair, swiveled it to face her and reached for his coffee. "I'll get to that program real soon now," he said comfortingly, "and then we'll be rolling in dough."

Real soon now, Jessica had learned the hard way, was computer jargon for an unspecified future when there was nothing more interesting to do. "Why don't you just say mañana and have done with it?" she asked.

Keir shook his head. "Jess, you wouldn't ask Picasso to stop in the middle of a masterpiece and paint the porch, would you?"

"Sometimes the porch needs paint."

"Feeling a little touchy this morning?" Brilliant sapphire eyes focused on her face. "How was your date last night?"

Jessica wanted to groan. In the six months she'd worked for him, Keir had asked about her dates perhaps half a dozen times. Even then, he had usually seemed not to be listening to the answer. But on this morning, of all mornings, he appeared to be intent.

She said coolly, "It was fine." At least, she told herself, it had been for about the first fifteen minutes, and the rest was none of his affair. "Is there some particular reason you're interested, or are you just grasping for any change of subject?"

He shrugged. "Randy told me that when you left yesterday you were glowing as if you'd swallowed a neon tube, so I figured you must have expected a really hot date. But I must say I don't see it myself—you just look like it was a very late night." He rolled his head back and forth as if his neck hurt.

Despite herself, Jessica felt a twinge of sympathy. "I could return that compliment. Did you work around the clock again?"

"I thought you wanted me to hurry up and finish this project so I can work on the real estate package."

"That would be a nice idea. How did your little business conference go?"

"Probably about as well as your date." His tone was perfectly calm. "The suits weren't the Mafia, after all, but they didn't seem to have anything profitable in mind, either—or even interesting. They just talked in circles about one of the programs I put up on the Internet last spring, and it took nearly an hour to get rid of them."

Jessica sighed. "Get rid of them? They had to want something, Keir, or they wouldn't have come."

"Well, whatever it was, they seemed more interested in dinner than in talking about it. But since I didn't have the whole evening to spend fiddling around with small talk—"

"They wanted to take you to dinner?" Jessica almost shrieked. "And you turned them down?"

"I was busy," Keir said reasonably.

Jessica felt as if she was talking to a kindergartner. "Don't you know anything about how the real world operates? Even my grandmother knew that more business was done over dinner tables than in boardrooms!"

"Is that a fact?" He actually sounded interested. "I thought they were just hungry, and since I didn't happen to be, and I still had this program to finish debugging—"

"Keir, you need a keeper! Or someone to teach you diplomacy, at least. Mail order is fine—it's keeping this place afloat. But if Toolshop is going to grow, you'll have to change your style in order to click with clients on a more personal level."

Keir was frowning.

Jessica plunged on. "People might secretly admire iconoclasts, but they don't do much business with them. They'll seek out people like themselves instead, ones they can be comfortable with."

"That makes sense. I'd much rather work with people like me than ones like the real estate person. Maybe I should call him—"

"That's not the right way to look at it! If you mess around with him much longer, he'll go looking for somebody who'll talk his language."

"Even if he doesn't get as good a result?"

"He probably won't know the difference. Half of success in business is learning to play the game, Keir. It's things like dressing right and knowing how to behave in all the awkward situations both in and out of the office, and—and even flattering the client's daughter if that's what it takes!"

She stopped abruptly, realizing that Keir was staring at her as if she'd grown a horn in the center of her forehead.

"Is that a quotation from the sayings of Chairman McIntyre?" he asked calmly.

Jessica bit her lip. She felt like a parrot, even though what she'd said was no less true just because Trevor also believed it. But she might as well talk to the wind as try to convince Keir.

She took a deep breath. "All right—whatever the suits might have wanted, the opportunity's gone now. But as long as I've got your attention, what do you plan to do about this cash crunch?"

Keir sighed. "Jess, you know money questions cramp my style. That's why I hired you, to keep the pressure off me when I'm doing important things." He waved a hand at the computer screen.

"I suppose we don't have to talk about it right this minute," she admitted reluctantly, "but—"

''If that means you're going to keep bringing it up every time you walk in, we might as well get it over with. I presume you have some suggestions?''

Jessica moved a stack of papers. ''If you hate the business side of things so much, why don't you give up Toolshop and work for somebody else?''

Keir looked horrified. ''And spend the next thirty years of my life tweaking programs that figure the odds of somebody dying or add up compound interest for banks? Jess, my brain would mildew. I'd—''

''All right, I see your point. But what's so important about this thing?'' She waved a hand at the screen, which was still mindlessly scrolling code. ''What does it do, anyway?''

''Do you really want me to explain it?''

''No,'' Jessica said hastily. ''Forget I asked. What I really want to know is if it has any commercial applications.''

''Oh, probably—when it's done.''

''And when is that likely to be? We could use the income right now.''

''Money wouldn't roll in for long if the program doesn't work.''

There was no arguing with that. ''Well—if we have no immediate way to increase income, the only other possibility is to cut expenses.'' She looked at her hands, then at him. ''Like salaries.''

Keir's jaw tightened. ''If you're suggesting I fire Randy and teach you to duplicate the software—''

''I'm not, actually.''

''Because I won't do it. The kid needs a safe place to go, and playing with the computer keeps him out of trouble.''

Jessica hadn't looked at it that way—but then, she didn't know anything about Randy's home and his background. She wondered just how much Keir knew, and how he'd discovered it.

Keir shifted in his chair, and Jessica was surprised to see a tinge of color rise in his face as if he was embarrassed. "Besides," he added gruffly, "I wouldn't trust you to turn that old computer on without blowing yourself up."

Jessica bristled. "I only crashed that computer once, Keir. And if you'd left it alone, I wouldn't have done that."

"I was simply improving the system."

"Right. It was so improved that it took a week to get it to run again at all."

"And you think that's *my* fault? If you weren't computer illiterate—"

Jessica put her chin up. "So maybe it's me you should get rid of instead of Randy."

Too late, she remembered that wasn't at all the way she'd planned to approach the subject. She was practically asking to be fired—and that was hardly a wise move for a woman who needed a job as desperately as she did just now.

"You?" Astonishment swept over Keir's face. "Why would I want to do that? Get rid of my lucky charm, my amulet—"

"Don't forget mascot," she said dryly, but she couldn't help feeling relieved.

"I haven't. And firing you isn't an option."

"Believe me, I appreciate that."

"In fact, I was thinking just the other day of offering you some kind of profit-sharing plan."

"Great idea. The only thing missing is the profit. You might as well be realistic, Keir. If it wasn't for my paycheck, the cash flow problems around here wouldn't be nearly so bad. And I've got things in order now so it would be fairly easy to keep the bookkeeping current. I could probably teach Randy the system, and you could just extend his hours a little and—''

Keir interrupted. ''Are you telling me you want to leave?''

Jessica hesitated. ''I don't want to, exactly.'' It was true, she thought. She was just a little uncomfortable about the idea of going to work somewhere else—but that must simply be a natural reaction to the challenge of seeking a different job and getting to know a new organization and a new employer. It certainly wasn't that Toolshop had been a perfect place to work, or Keir a perfect boss.

''Then why tell me all this?''

She took a deep breath and launched herself on the explanation she'd worked out in the wee hours of the morning. ''I've done a lot of thinking lately, and I want to better myself. I told you when I took the job that I didn't expect to stay forever, and now that I have some work experience, other employers will consider hiring me.''

Keir frowned.

Hastily, she added, ''Please don't think I don't appreciate what you've done for me, Keir. But I have to be realistic, and I have to look out for the future. I really need to make more money in order to provide for myself, and I know you can't pay it. But I want to be fair to you, because you took a big chance on me. So I thought I should tell you up front that I'm going to start looking for another job.''

Keir whistled, long and low. ''So Randy was wrong.''

''About what?''

''That glow of yours. The rising executive didn't propose last night.''

''Randy didn't know a thing about Trev—'' Jessica clapped a hand over her mouth, but it was too late.

"No. He didn't," Keir agreed. "He just said you walked out of here looking like a resistor with too much electricity running through it, and since you were going out with McIntyre and obviously had something to celebrate, I figured that must be what it was. But I can't see you being so worried about money if the rising executive came through, so—"

To her utter disgust, Jessica's eyes suddenly brimmed with tears. Even through the blurriness, she could see the compassion in Keir's face, and that made the tears start to overflow.

"Tell Papa all about it," he murmured and leaned forward to hand her a big white handkerchief.

Jessica sniffed. "My grandmother taught me that a lady never cries in public."

"Since we're not exactly overrun with customers this morning, I don't think her standard applies in this case."

"Yes, it does. Grandmother's definition of public included any audience at all." Jessica blotted the corners of her eyes with the folded edge of the handkerchief, being careful of her mascara. "And in any case, you're not paying me to weep over my love life, so—" She jumped up.

Keir lounged deeper into his chair. "Just consider it a fringe benefit of working here."

The sudden motion of standing made Jessica's head spin, and she reached out blindly for support. She didn't even see Keir move, but instantly he was there beside her, his arm around her waist, taking her weight against the length of his body.

She'd never been so close to him before, and even in her sudden dizziness she found herself thinking how solid he was, and how strong. He was the only thing holding her upright, and she felt tiny and helpless as she leaned against him, her face almost buried in the sweet-smelling wool of his favorite gray sweater. How, she wondered, had he built up those hard muscles? Did the man take secret breaks to pump iron?

Her head still felt fuzzy, and the room looked as if it had a slight orange cast. Keir held her a few inches away from him and looked speculatively at her face. "When was the last time you ate anything?"

She tried to remember, but the only thing she could think of was the pastrami sandwich that had been yesterday's lunch. "A while."

"Well, no wonder you're a bit disconnected today, if you've been skipping meals. Come on." He shifted his grip and walked her toward the door as if she were a rag doll.

"You're a fine one to talk," Jessica muttered. "You think peanut butter, banana and jelly on bread makes a balanced meal."

"Why not? It's protein, fruit, carbohydrates and starch. You could do worse." He pulled the money box from one of the file drawers in her desk and opened it. "I see what you mean about a cash flow crisis."

"There are a couple of checks to go to the bank, but... Keir, you can't just take that, it's company funds."

"So I'll put in an IOU. Anyway, if we're down to our last twenty bucks, we might as well blow it, too, and have it over with." He didn't sound at all concerned.

The bracing chill of the wind brought some color to Jessica's face, and by the time they crossed the street to the deli she was no longer dizzy. "I'm feeling better. There's really no need to pamper me."

Keir didn't pause. "You need to eat, anyway. When a woman is in a delicate condition—"

It took a moment before his words registered. "What do you mean, *a delicate condition*?" Jessica sputtered. "If that's some Victorian way of asking if I'm *pregnant*—" Her voice failed.

He held the door for her and ushered her to a table, then went to the counter without a word.

Jessica sat down with a thud.

A couple of minutes later Keir set a cheese Danish and a glass of orange juice in front of her and took the chair opposite, propping his elbows on the table. "Well?" he said matter-of-factly. "Are you?"

"No! And where you ever got the idea I might be—"

"It's perfectly logical. First there's your sudden concern about the future. Second, that was a fantastic attempt to faint. Third, I seem to have heard that sudden tears and a loss of appetite are common phenomena in early pregnancy. Therefore, it seemed reasonable to conclude that your glow yesterday was due to the great news you had for the rising executive. Only he didn't think it was such great news, so now you're worried about taking care of yourself and looking out for the future—"

Jessica gritted her teeth. "You're logical, all right. You're also dead wrong, but I don't suppose that bothers you much."

"So eat your Danish and tell me what did happen."

She considered while she broke the Danish into bite-size pieces. Some explanation was obviously necessary, but what was the minimum Keir would settle for? "You know all that stuff I was spouting a while ago about how to be successful in business? Or weren't you paying attention at all?"

"I vaguely recall some of it," Keir admitted.

"Well, I wouldn't expect any more than that. There's one other thing that comes in handy for a young man who wants to climb the corporate ladder—besides the right clothes, the right car, the right haircut and the right attitude toward his superiors." She had to swallow hard and steady her voice before she could finish. "The right wife."

Keir frowned. "I don't quite see—"

"The trouble is, I fit the description almost perfectly. I can carry on a conversation with anyone, I can pour tea with the best grande dames, I can paint a perfectly adequate watercolor and ride a horse really well. I could probably write an etiquette book. And I'm a Bennington."

He looked puzzled. "That's important?"

"Oh, yes," she said wryly. "The Benningtons weren't the first settlers around here, but we had a big hand in turning it from a cow town into a real city. A Bennington provided a civilizing influence on every important board and committee in Kansas City for a hundred years, till we ran short of Benningtons and had to cut back. And as for social leverage—well, the Benningtons were too elite to move to newer neighborhoods where we might have to mingle with the upstarts. We stayed right in the family mansion on Ward Parkway."

Keir shrugged. "So what's the hitch? If you're so perfect—"

"*Almost* perfect," Jessica corrected. "There's the little matter of money. We ran short of that along the way, too."

"Ah." He nodded. "Now I understand. Creating the image of success doesn't come cheap, and some extra principal would be very handy for the rising executive just now."

"I suppose you could even call it venture capital." A tinge of bitterness crept into Jessica's voice. She toyed with her Danish, unwilling to look at Keir.

"Is that why you're going job-hunting?" he asked finally. "To look for a place that will pay you enough to make the rising executive change his mind?"

Jessica stared at him, astonished. Did Keir really think she was idiot enough to continue to chase after a man to whom she was so clearly unimportant? He certainly looked somber.

"No," she said, keeping her expression utterly deadpan. "It would take much more than that, I'm afraid. I suppose I'll just have to hope that I'll trip over the pot of gold at the end of the rainbow—but failing that, I don't have any choice but to be noble about it and make the sacrifice." The irony in her voice shaded into bitterness despite her best efforts. Annoyed by her loss of control, Jessica pushed her plate away and stood up. "Don't you think we'd better go back to work, just in case there are some customers today?"

Keir looked as if he'd like to argue the point, but without a word he shoved his chair back and followed her.

The front door of Toolshop Software was standing ajar, and the moment Jessica realized it her heart sank to her toes. "There's someone inside," she whispered.

Keir shook his head. "I doubt it. I didn't lock the door when we left, so it probably just blew open."

"You left the place standing open with all those valuable computers inside?"

"Jess, the newest one is a year old—it's practically antique. Which reminds me, I need to give Bernie a call. He can get a bulk price on a preview model of the next generation."

"And how are you planning to pay for it?"

Keir didn't seem to hear. "The new processor should speed my work up by a hundred percent."

As he put a hand on the doorknob, Jessica seized his arm. The question of a new computer was suddenly forgotten. Her thoughts had snapped to the ones he already owned. "Keir, the average thief won't know or care if a computer's new or old. And if somebody's in there robbing the place right now and you go charging in, you could be hurt!"

He grinned. "Fancy that! You sound as if you'd miss me." He pushed the door wide.

Further protest would do no good. Did the man have no sense? "Of course I'd miss you," Jessica said tartly. "You haven't signed my latest paycheck yet. And there's a little matter of a recommendation, too...."

Keir stopped suddenly on the threshold, and Jessica ran into his back and nearly bowled herself over. Almost absentmindedly, he reached around and steadied her, drawing her close to his side in the doorway. Jessica saw what had made him pause and had to stifle a gasp.

Two of yesterday's mysterious visitors were standing in the center of the small reception room, looking awkward. The third—the man who had given Jessica his card—was leaning over her desk and looking at the day's calendar.

"Excuse me," Keir told him. "But that's a private area, and I'd appreciate it if—"

Jessica jabbed him with her elbow. Keir released his breath with a whoosh and was quiet.

Swallowing her annoyance at the visitor's nosiness, Jessica stepped forward with a smile. "We're terribly sorry to keep you waiting, but we had to step out to attend to some customer service matters. Is there something we can help you with?"

Keir's eyes sparkled. "Is *that* how it's done?" he murmured. "I'd have called it apple polishing, myself, but I suppose you know best."

Jessica glared at him. "Coffee, anyone? I'll make a fresh pot and bring it in." The three visitors looked doubtfully from her to Keir and back.

Keir finally took the hint and crossed the room to the door of his office. "If you'd like to come in, gentlemen . . ."

It took Jessica a few minutes to locate enough cups, but by the time she tapped on the door and carried the tray in, the ice had obviously not yet been broken. The three visitors had seated themselves in a row on the bedraggled couch. Today the suits were navy blue and the ties burgundy. Jessica thought they looked almost like the three monkeys representing see no evil, hear no evil and speak no evil.

Keir seemed perfectly at ease, leaning back in his chair with his fingers tented together. He got up when Jessica came in, however, and tried to clear a corner of his desk for the coffee. "I hope you appreciate this service," he said over his shoulder to the suits. "She's a Bennington, you know." He grinned at Jessica like a student proud of the lesson he'd learned.

She stifled a groan and went to her desk.

She could hear the murmur of voices now and then through the thin door of the inner office, but even if she'd been trying to listen, she couldn't have picked up the words. She wasn't sure she'd have wanted to overhear the conversation, anyway. Listening to Keir's idea of buttering up a customer would probably give her an ulcer.

It was half an hour before the door opened. Not long enough, Jessica calculated, for any serious business. Not that she'd expected any, of course.

The three suits trod silently across the outer office, almost in lockstep, and went out before Jessica could find her voice. It was probably just as well, she concluded, since she didn't have a clue what to say. Thanking them didn't seem quite appropriate, since she had no idea what they'd wanted in the first place, and as for inviting them to come back...

The office door was still open. From her desk, she could see Keir's feet propped on his workstation atop the computer case.

Her eyes widened at the sight. What on earth had happened in there to make him treat a computer with such disrespect? She paused in the doorway, half afraid of what she would see.

Keir had slouched in his chair and was staring at the ceiling as if he'd never seen it before.

''Keir?'' she said hesitantly.

''Did you know the cracks up there look like a map of the Nile Delta?''

''What happened?''

Almost dreamily, he turned his head and gave her an angelic smile. ''I have tripped over the pot of gold at the end of the rainbow,'' he said. ''Or at least, I've been given a very good glimpse of where it lies.''

''Are you feeling all right?'' Half-consciously she moved toward him as if to lay her hand on his forehead.

''Oh, yes.'' Keir jumped up and seized her hand. ''How about it, Jess? What's it worth to you to have half of it for yourself?''

CHAPTER THREE

HE DIDN'T *look* feverish, Jessica thought, but he certainly *sounded* as if he was delirious. "Do you want to tell me about it?" she asked, trying to sound casual.

Keir guided her to the end of the couch, and, grasping her hand between both of his, kicked his chair around so he could perch on the edge of the seat. "If we handle it right," he confided, "we can make enough money on this deal to set us both up for life. I'll never have to listen to anybody fuss about cash flow again, and you can afford anything your little heart desires—including the rising executive."

As if she'd still want Trevor... But Jessica dismissed that thought the instant it crossed her mind. She didn't owe Keir any additional explanations, and there were far more important things demanding her concentration just now. "Would you take it from the top, Keir? At the moment I don't know if you were just offered a surefire investment in a diamond mine or a job as a hired killer. And before I agree to get involved in *anything,* I'd sort of like to know what it is."

"Jess, darling, do you think I'd drag you into something as foolish as investing in a diamond mine?"

He hadn't said anything about the hired killing, though, she noted.

"Besides, if neither you nor Toolshop has any money," he went on offhandedly, "what would we invest?"

"Well, that's a comfort." Jessica's voice was dry. "For a minute there, I was starting to worry that you'd gotten into something *impractical*. So who did you agree to kill? And are you going to use poison, or just annoy the victim to death by refusing to explain the way your mind works?''

"What? You're making no sense at all, Jess. If you'll just give me a chance to tell you what happened . . .''

"That's what I'm waiting for." He was still holding her hand, Jessica realized belatedly. She drew it away and folded her arms across her chest.

"The three suits,'' Keir began, "represent Softek—''

Jessica frowned. "That wasn't the name on the business card.''

"Who's telling this story, you or me? Softek is—what? The second-largest developer of computer software in the country?''

"You expect me to keep track? I just know Toolshop isn't exactly in the same league.''

"Maybe they're third—but anyway, they're right at the top. You wouldn't expect them to go around openly announcing that they're unhappy with their own research and development department and they're looking for free-lance ideas, would you?''

Jessica shook her head in confusion. "Is that what those men told you?''

"Not in so many words, no. I was reading between the lines for that part. In an effort to keep the negotiations under wraps, Softek sent the suits—who are ostensibly from an engineering research firm—to talk to me about my new approach to maximizing the—''

Jessica interrupted. "Keir, you are not only incapable of reading between the lines, most of the time you don't have the slightest idea where the lines *are*. But you're right about one thing. This whole scheme is a pot of gold at the rainbow's end, so I'd suggest that before you start spending the windfall, you give a little thought to—''

Keir's voice cut firmly across hers. "Softek wants to buy the rights to the high-memory management program I put out on the Internet last spring."

There was no doubting the conviction in his voice, but she still had her doubts. "They actually said so?"

"Straight out, in exactly those words."

Well, Jessica thought, that changed things. She had only the vaguest understanding of what that particular bit of software actually did. All she knew was that it had something to do with exactly how information was stored in a computer's memory. Keir had once attempted to explain it to her, but when he'd started into the algorithms, Jessica had told him in desperation that if she had to understand the thing in order to use it, she'd take a good old filing cabinet instead. Keir had simply shaken his head in disappointment and gone back to work.

Still, Jessica had no trouble picturing the kind of deal he was talking about, and suddenly her brain was clicking almost as efficiently as the computer. Keir might be overstating the case a bit. The deal probably wouldn't set them up for life, but there could be licensing fees and royalties on top of a flat payment—enough to make Toolshop profitable for several years to come.

We'll need a good lawyer, she reflected, and paused with a frown. *We?* What was she thinking?

"Wait a minute," she said, almost unwillingly. "If they want to buy your program, where do I come into it? You did the work. If you'd like to give me a nice little bonus when it's all done, I certainly wouldn't turn it down—but I don't quite see why you're offering me half."

For the first time since she'd come into the office, Keir looked a little uncomfortable. He shifted in his chair and looked at the ceiling again.

Jessica almost felt sympathetic. It was no wonder, she thought, that in his excitement he'd said more than he'd intended. Now the poor guy probably thought she'd taken his offer seriously and that she'd be heartbroken if he backed out. As if she'd hold him to it!

"Well, you see, Jess," he said, sounding a little awkward, "it's sort of a package deal. And that means I need you more than ever."

Jessica tapped her foot on the carpet and stared at him. For a full minute, the silence in the office was broken only by the patient hum of the computer. Keir showed no inclination to explain. "What kind of a package?" Jessica asked finally.

Keir waved a hand at the computer screen. "They liked the looks of my new idea, too."

"The one you've been debugging?"

"They're going to hire me to explore all the possibilities, with the goal of expanding it into a commercial product and in the next five years making it a necessary accessory to every personal computer sold in the world."

Jessica blinked in surprise. She'd never doubted Keir's talent, but it sounded as if Softek had decided he was one of the generation's geniuses. "Now I really don't see why you need me. If you think I'd be any use with that sort of work..."

"Of course not, Jess. You'd be no help at all with the technical stuff." He leaned back in his chair, apparently comfortable once more.

"Well, you don't need to be insulting—" Jessica interrupted herself in mid-thought. "Wait a minute. You said just this morning that you don't want to work for anybody else."

"I said I didn't want to spend my life making niggling little adjustments to stupid bookkeeping programs. But to get paid to do what I'd be doing anyway—"

"Fiddling with this program?"

"Exactly."

"I thought you said it was almost ready to go."

"In a preliminary form, yes. But if I had another year to play with it, I'd have a much better product. As a part of Softek I'd have those extra months, and the backing to make my idea the industry standard instead of just another cute little innovation produced by a hacker in his spare time."

"And I wouldn't be nagging you to sell copies for whatever they would bring in order to keep Toolshop afloat in the meantime," Jessica mused. "You've got a point. But—"

"I thought you'd see the sense in it. If I play my cards right, I think I can go in as chief programmer."

"Supervising a bunch of other people?" Jessica was horrified. "Keir, you'd be a dead loss at that, and if some disgruntled employee didn't stab you in the back before the first month was out, you'd jump off the top of the building in despair!"

"No, no. It's a courtesy title, though not a very well-chosen one. Chief programmers don't supervise other people. They sit in quiet corner offices, think abstract thoughts and pursue great ideas without concern about whether the results are immediately practical. And that's what I do best."

Jessica could hardly argue with that.

"Besides," he added, "it would be a *warm* corner office, and you couldn't hassle me about how I was going to pay for my new computers."

He made it sound as if her financial concerns were completely frivolous, but Jessica was so used to that attitude that she let it pass without comment. "I still don't completely understand why you think you need me at all. Am I supposed to guard your office door and protect you from the corporate vultures while you think these great thoughts?"

He looked a bit uncomfortable again. "Something like that, but—"

"Well, in that case, don't think I'm going to let you off easily. My price for scaring off vultures is a nice title and—"

Keir grinned. "I have one in mind, as a matter of fact."

"And a decent raise. But I won't hold you up for half of the profits."

"No, I said half, and I meant half. You'll be earning it, believe me."

She watched him warily. "All right, now I really want the details. If Softek wants you badly enough to give you all this freedom, surely—"

"You see," Keir said simply, "at the moment they don't know they want me."

Jessica looked at him for a long moment and started to rub her temples. Keir had given her headaches before, but this one was turning into a champion. "They don't know they want to hire you? Keir, for heaven's sake, exactly what did they say?"

"The suits were fascinated by the idea, and they're going back to talk to the head man about it. I think they're going to offer to buy it outright—so it will be up to us to convince them that I'm the only one who can pull the project together and make it sing."

The computer hummed. Jessica's head throbbed. Almost to herself, she said, "I keep thinking the other shoe has dropped and there can't be any more surprises—but you're turning out to be a centipede."

Keir smiled as sunnily as if she'd paid him a compliment. "You're the one who gave me the idea, Jess."

She shook her head. "I can't imagine how you came to that conclusion."

"It was that lecture you gave me this morning about getting along in the business world—how important it is to impress clients and all that sort of thing. Well, it's just as true when it comes to impressing a boss, isn't it?''

"I suppose so," Jessica said carefully. She could sense a chasm yawning at her feet, but she couldn't quite see in what direction it lay.

"And even more so when he's a *prospective* boss, wouldn't you say?"

"It depends on the boss."

"Precisely." Keir's tone was approving. "You may have heard that Softek was recently purchased by a tycoon."

Jessica nodded. "Walter Wyatt. There was a profile of him in one of the magazines last month."

"I read it, too. He made his money in manufacturing gizmos, and computers are an entirely new line for him. He's a corporate sort, not a regular computer guy, so he no doubt puts great stock in all those things you were telling me about this morning. I guess that's why the suits left yesterday without ever getting down to business—they didn't seem to think I'd fit in with the new order at Softek."

He seemed wounded at the idea. Jessica tried not to smile.

"Of course, they came back," he went on, "which is why I'm convinced we can pull this off. They were quite impressed with you, too. They even said it was too bad you weren't the one in charge. So I was thinking—"

"You want me to front for you? Represent myself as your negotiator or something?"

"Not exactly. For one thing, you couldn't possibly pull it off, Jess—the first time someone asked a question about the program, you'd fall apart. But since nobody introduced you today, the suits don't know you're my secretary."

"Isn't it obvious? My desk's out there, yours is here. I brought in the coffee—"

"I mean, they don't know you're *just* my secretary. So when I take you to meet Walter Wyatt this weekend—"

"Why would I want to meet Walter—"

"He'll take one look at you, with your Bennington class and style and gorgeous looks, and think that if I had the good sense to recognize all that, I'm exactly his sort."

He looked quite pleased with himself, which made Jessica so nervous that she hardly noticed the compliment.

"After all," Keir went on, "any man you'd marry must be something special."

Jessica swallowed hard. "I beg your pardon, but my ears are buzzing so loudly I don't think I heard you right. Any man I'd *what*?"

"Marry." Keir enunciated it very clearly.

"Oh, no. I may have said some things about the right wife being an important consideration in the corporate world, but I hardly think that applies to you."

He looked disappointed. "Why not? What's the problem?"

"Oh, nothing much," Jessica drawled. "It's just a minor detail. I have absolutely no desire to marry you, Keir."

"I know that." He sounded a little disgusted. "Who said anything about actually getting married?"

"You did. Unless you mean this would just be an act till you get your deal nailed down."

"I never thought you were dim, Jess. We don't have to get married, just pretend to be firmly engaged." He frowned. "Of course, being married would be a lot better. It looks more permanent, you know. But marriages leave records, and a wedding date sometime this week would look a little suspicious, don't you think?"

"You amaze me," Jessica said. "Why not just break into the official computers and backdate the marriage license?"

Keir considered the question briefly then shook his head. "No, those things are pretty well protected. It could take a couple of weeks just to figure out the password."

He sounded perfectly serious. Of course, Jessica thought, that was the trouble with concrete, logical, mathematical minds. Keir probably wouldn't recognize irony if it bit him in the nose.

"Engagements, on the other hand, can happen any time," Keir went on. "We could have been engaged for months, and nobody can prove differently."

Jessica didn't bother to point out that there were plenty of people who knew there was nothing between the two of them but a paycheck. Since those folks didn't move in Walter Wyatt's circles, any danger he'd find out was slight.

She wondered if *she* was the one who was delirious. The whole thing was beginning to sound reasonable.

Keir seemed to recognize she was wavering. "Think of the money, Jess," he wheedled. "You could sail around the world. You could retire at—how old are you, anyway?"

"Twenty-five," she said absently.

"You could buy... I'm sorry, I meant to say you could marry the rising executive. I'm not talking about a small piece of change, you know." He reached for her hand. "What have you got to lose?"

Jessica looked him over as closely as if she'd never seen him before. His hair was wilder than usual this morning. The springy dark curls looked as if he hadn't bothered with a comb after his shower. But a good cut would go a long way toward getting that under control. As for his clothes—everything the man wore would have to go. But he was tall and well-built, and a good tailor could take care of the rest with no trouble at all. With just a little effort devoted to his appearance, he could put most men in the shade. Taming his tongue might be a little more difficult....

"The first thing is to get you out of those jeans," she mused.

Keir's eyes widened. "Jess! I hardly expected you'd get *that* far into the spirit of things. But of course if you think it's a good idea—"

Belatedly, she heard the double meaning in her words, and tried in vain to fight the embarrassed color flooding her cheeks.

Keir seemed to be tickled. "And here I assumed a Bennington would never blush, no matter what," he murmured. "But that just goes to prove what I know about high society, doesn't it?"

"And into a nice business suit," she said firmly, trying to pretend he hadn't interrupted. "That sweater will have to go, too."

"This?" He peered at his chest as if he'd forgotten what he was wearing. Jessica thought he probably had. "I can't throw this away, Jess. I get all my best ideas while I'm wearing this sweater."

"Well, if the notion ever crosses your mind to give it to a panhandler, that would be the single best idea you've had in your whole life. Of course, finding a panhandler who's willing to take it would be the real challenge."

Keir leaned forward. "So, it's a deal?"

Jessica considered. As he'd said, what did she have to lose? The idea was wild enough that it just might pay off. And, in case the rainbow he was chasing proved elusive after all—well, nothing was keeping her from starting her job search in the meantime, was it? She couldn't end up any worse off.

"It's a deal," she said, and solemnly shook his hand. Somehow, the words felt like a vow.

* * *

With the decision made, Keir's attention immediately wandered to the computer. Jessica thought he was probably unaware that even though he was still talking to her, his fingertips were caressing the keyboard as if it was his lover's skin.

There was something wrong with that image, though. In fact, he seemed to find the computer a more fascinating mistress than any mere woman could be. The idea didn't bother Jessica. The last thing they'd need in the midst of this crazy masquerade would be for Keir to stumble across a woman and fall in love.

She excused herself to return to her work, and before she was out of the office he was again absorbed in the intricacies of his program. More than once before the morning was gone, Jessica envied him his powers of concentration. Her attention was fragmented, and she found herself watching the clock, unable to believe it wasn't even time for lunch yet.

Just as she was about to interrupt Keir to see if he wanted his usual bologna sandwich, his door opened. She was surprised to see he'd put on a coat over the disreputable sweater and was tossing his car keys from one hand to the other.

"I'm going over to see Bernie," he announced cheerfully. "It might take a while, so just go to lunch whenever you like—I doubt there will be customers standing in line when you get back."

Eating was the furthest thing from Jessica's mind. "Are you planning to buy that new computer? Because I don't think this would be a good time at all."

"Jess, honey, if you're trying to remind me of why we're launching this scheme, you couldn't choose a better way. But as a matter of fact, I'm not buying today, I'm selling."

"Selling what?" she asked suspiciously.

"Bernie's been trying to talk me out of my first-generation original personal computer for two years now. I'm going to sell it to him."

"Why?"

"Jess, what's wrong with you? We have to have seed money. You said yourself that the image of success doesn't come cheap."

"You told me once that computer belongs in a museum."

Keir shrugged. "It does, but in the meantime the thing's just taking up space and collecting dust in my office."

"What's Bernie going to do with it?"

"Tear it up for parts, probably. But that's none of my business anymore."

"But you love that computer," she said uncertainly.

"Well, sometimes you have to be noble about it and make the sacrifice."

He'd quoted her own words back at her. The only difference was that she'd been talking about Trevor—and she hadn't meant a syllable of what she said. While Keir, on the other hand . . .

He was almost out the door when she called, "Keir, you haven't given me any details about this meeting with Walter Wyatt."

"It's a party Saturday at his house. I'll tell you about it over dinner tonight."

"Dinner?"

"Isn't that what the Benningtons call it?"

"Honestly, Keir—"

"I assume we'll need a rehearsal or two before the big event. Don't you agree? You might be thinking about an appropriate place to go."

"Well, that depends. Will I have to teach you to use the correct fork?"

"Jess, darling..." A sudden look of concern crossed his face. "What's a fork?"

He was gone before she could throw something at him.

This, Jessica thought, might not have been such a good idea after all.

It was mid-afternoon before he came back, smiling and relaxed. Jessica felt a flush of relief. He'd been gone far longer than such a simple deal should have required, and she'd spent the last hour contemplating all the things that could go wrong with this stunt. She'd had plenty of leisure to do so, since the day's mail had included not a single order.

Of course, she told herself wryly, it was a bit soon to be relieved. That smile of Keir's could simply mean that he'd forgotten all about the antique computer and bought the new one instead.

"I hope Bernie came through," she began, "because I made a reservation at Felicity's. It's on the expensive side, but if you're going to learn how things should be done, there's no substitute for quality."

"I'm glad to see you had faith in me." Keir pulled a crumpled wad of bills from his pocket.

Jessica's eyes widened. "I had no idea that piece of junk—I'm sorry, that old computer—would be worth so much."

"Oh, I didn't have to sell it, after all. I started out by telling Bernie all about my plan. He thought it was great and made me a loan instead, so I've still got the computer in reserve."

"A loan? What if we don't pull it off?"

Keir waggled a finger under her nose. "You'll have to start thinking more positively than that, Jess." He patted his pockets. "There was something else, too.... Oh, here it is." He pulled out a small envelope and dumped a ring onto the desk blotter in front of her.

Jessica watched as the gold band spun merrily and finally settled into stillness. It lay on the blotter at an angle, and the big green stone caught and fractured the light like an enormous eye. "What's this, Keir?"

He frowned. "Well, my best guess is it's an emerald, but—"

She glared at him. "I know it's an emerald, Keir. The question is, where did you get it?"

His face cleared. "Oh, it belonged to Bernie's grandmother."

"And he sold it to you?"

"Of course he didn't sell it to me. Do you think I'd use up our hard-to-find cash on an engagement ring?"

"Don't you mean Bernie's cash? If you're telling me you simply borrowed it from him—Keir, I can't possibly take responsibility for a ring like that. The stone must be a full carat, and it's a gorgeous shade of green. Emeralds like that one—"

"Don't grow on trees," Keir finished helpfully. "And don't worry, Bernie trusts you. When I told him you're a Bennington, he said you must know how to take care of toys like that, or they would have thrown you out of the family long ago." He picked up her left hand and slid the ring into position. "See? It even fits just right."

And, Jessica had to admit, it looked wonderful on her slim finger. The deep, rich green of the step-cut emerald was surrounded by sparkling baguette diamonds set in gold. It was exactly the sort of engagement ring she'd have chosen for herself.

She looked at Keir, intending to tell him to pass the word to Bernie that she'd be very careful with his grandmother's ring. But a split second later she'd forgotten what she'd been planning to say, for Keir was bending over her. His palm cupped her cheek, resting warmly against the soft skin, and his lips gently brushed hers.

There was a sudden all-gone feeling in the pit of Jessica's stomach, like the instant at the peak of a high dive when she was weightless, before gravity and momentum tugged her down and into the water.

His mouth was soft, his touch so sensitive that it was almost as if he was asking a question. As he drew back, Jessica said uncertainly, "Why did you do that?"

His voice was ever so slightly unsteady. "Because it seemed like a good idea. Now, I'm not so sure. Hi, Randy."

Jessica gasped. Randy was standing in the doorway with his mouth agape.

Keir settled comfortably on the corner of Jessica's desk. "Sorry to shock you," he told Randy. "I don't suppose you had any idea?"

Randy seemed to collect himself. "Sure." He was obviously making an effort to sound careless. "I figured out a long time ago that you guys were nuts about each other."

"You see?" Keir murmured. His lips were close to Jessica's ear, and his breath stirred her hair and sent a quiver through her sensitive scalp. "I told you people wouldn't question exactly when all this happened."

The maître d' happened to be at the front door of Felicity's when Keir's car pulled up. For just an instant, Jonathan's face showed shock. Then his self-control returned and his expression was once more suitably calm.

Of course, it was no wonder he'd been startled. Felicity's seldom saw a car as beat up as Keir's. The parking valet, who was obviously not as well-seasoned in his job as Jonathan, made a face as he slid behind the wheel.

Jonathan stepped forward to hold the door. "Miss Bennington, how good to see you again so soon! Mr.—''

Keir grabbed the maître d's hand and shook it briskly. "Saunders is the name," he said. "I'm glad to meet you."

"My pleasure, sir," Jonathan said. Jessica thought he sounded as if he'd bitten into a lemon.

Jessica didn't blame him. She was pretty well mortified herself. She held her tongue till Jonathan had seated them in the most reclusive, private area Felicity's boasted, and as soon as he was gone she leaned toward Keir. "Why did you introduce yourself to Jonathan?"

Keir shrugged. "So he'd know my name next time."

"Believe me, it wasn't necessary. A good maître d' picks up names from the reservations list, or from the credit card at the end of the evening—and he never forgets."

"But you made the reservations," Keir pointed out. "And I don't use credit cards."

Jessica bit her tongue. "Well, please don't do it again."

"You mean I should just pretend the headwaiter knows me and try to pass myself off as a regular, even if I've never been in the place before?"

"There's a difference between giving your name and acting as if you'd been fraternity brothers, all right?"

"Isn't that a little uppity?"

"It's a question of respect—for him as much as yourself."

"Okay, I've got it. I'll just pretend he was my butler once upon a time and treat him accordingly."

"Keir, have you ever seen a butler?"

"You mean besides in the movies?"

Jessica sighed. "That's what I thought."

"Anyway, he knew your name. So why shouldn't he know mine?"

"Believe me," she said dryly, "he'll remember yours, too, next time you come in. And he knows me because I've been coming here since I was a child."

"Well, that makes sense. Of course Benningtons wouldn't stoop to patronizing fast-food joints. Did they make French fries for you here, or did you have to eat snails with the adults?" Keir took the wine list the steward offered, glanced at it and smiled winningly. "I don't have a clue," he said. "So how about bringing one from column A and one from column B?" He handed the list to the stunned steward and put his elbows on the table. "Now," he said, "what was it you were going to teach me tonight, Jess?"

Jessica sighed. It didn't take a lot of intuition to know that this was going to be a very long evening.

CHAPTER FOUR

THE wine steward cleared his throat and said, "Perhaps, sir, if you could tell me what dishes you and the lady will be enjoying this evening, I could recommend a wine you might fancy."

Jessica didn't blame the steward for his reluctance to put his reputation on the line. She suspected that even if he brought out Dom Perignon, Keir was capable of telling him it tasted like battery acid. But she thought she saw a faint sneer on the steward's face, and she couldn't help resenting his superior attitude.

Over the past couple of years—ever since Clementine's death had wrought such a tremendous change in her circumstances—Jessica had had a lot of practice at detecting slights, and this one set her antenna quivering. Keir might be ignorant about wine, but he certainly wasn't stupid, and it wasn't the steward's job to make him feel inadequate.

But perhaps she was overreacting, she told herself. She'd never encountered any problem of the sort at Felicity's before. The respect the staff showed despite her changed circumstances was one of the reasons she liked the place so well, and it was why she'd chosen it tonight. And Keir hadn't seemed to notice anything wrong. In fact he was smiling at the steward.

"I can probably make a guess about what I'll *order*," he said, "but I'd say the *enjoyment* part depends entirely on the skills of the cook."

"Chef," Jessica said. She couldn't help it; she'd already bitten her tongue till it hurt. She turned to the steward. "How about bringing a nice rosé? I'm sure you have a vintage that will go with almost anything."

The steward sniffed and hurried away.

Jessica toyed with her napkin and said, "I need a hundred dollars from that stash of yours, Keir."

He reached into his pocket. "You mean for the wine?" He tossed a crisp bill onto the table. "It had better be good, at that price."

She shook her head.

"Clothes?" he guessed. "You've been looking at my necktie as if you don't like it, you know."

"Well, I've never seen one printed with microchip circuits before."

"Haven't you?" Keir flipped the end of the tie up to look at it more closely. "Bernie said they were all the rage when he gave me this for Christmas."

"We'll have to do something about the matter of clothes by Saturday night, that's sure. You can't wear that to Walter Wyatt's party."

"But I like this tie."

Jessica didn't doubt it. "That's not why I want the hundred, though. I'm going to use it to bribe Jonathan."

"You're going to pay the pseudo butler a C-note? Whatever for?"

"To give you lessons in how to conduct yourself so wine stewards won't sneer at you. If he succeeds, it'll be well worth it—because I can see already that you're far beyond my feeble talents."

"And you a Bennington, too." Keir sounded rather sad. "I thought nothing would be beyond you." He turned to look for Jonathan, who was seating a couple nearby, and waved him over.

The maître d' paused beside the table. "Yes, sir?"

"The lady has a proposition for you," Keir said expansively, and held up the folded hundred-dollar bill between two fingers. "She wants to pay you to teach me how to impress your wine steward."

The maître d's face was a study, Jessica thought. She'd never seen so many conflicting emotions on one face all at the same time. Jonathan seemed to be experiencing a mixture of bewilderment and shock, along with the fascination of a bird who'd been mesmerized by the gaze of a cobra.

The offer seemed to strike him completely speechless, as well, for he was still simply standing there when the wine steward returned with a bottle.

The steward's slight smirk died when he spotted Jonathan, and he stepped to the table with an exaggerated air of concern. "Will this be acceptable, sir?" he asked Keir, displaying the label.

Keir barely glanced at it before he took the bottle out of the steward's hands. "It'll do. But be a good fellow and go get me an opener, will you?"

Jonathan choked and said, in a strangled voice, "Allow me, sir."

Jessica closed her eyes in pain, and kept them closed all through the little tasting ritual. She'd have plugged her ears, too, if she could have done so without being obvious.

"Jess," Keir said finally, "you can come out now."

Reluctantly, she opened her eyes.

The steward and Jonathan were gone, and Keir was watching her over his upraised glass. "This doesn't taste half bad, actually. It doesn't hold a candle to a really good draft beer, but—"

She picked up her glass. "I heard Jonathan call it a friendly little wine."

"It's a good thing it knows how to mind its manners," he said solemnly, "because I would never stand for one that was rude. Especially if it decided to be rude to you."

Suddenly a bubble of laughter rose in Jessica's throat. Whatever else Keir was, he was certainly an original, sublimely at ease with himself no matter what anyone else thought. "The look on Jonathan's face," she managed to say, "was worth the hundred dollars—even if he hadn't taught you anything at all about wine."

Very slowly, as if he'd had to think about it first, Keir began to smile.

She'd never noticed before that his whole face got into the act. Not only did his eyes light with a brilliance that was almost painful, but the tanned skin around them crinkled merrily, and deep laugh lines appeared around his mouth. He was really stunningly attractive when he smiled. . . .

Confusion swept over Jessica, and she reached hastily for her menu. "What kinds of things do you like to eat? Besides bologna and peanut butter, I mean."

"As long as you don't make me eat snails or raw fish, I'm open to almost anything."

"Oh, Keir, sushi's really wonderful when it's properly prepared. I had some in San Francisco once—"

"After we hit the jackpot I'll let you take me there," he said firmly. "But in the meantime, since this isn't San Francisco, I think I'll stick with beef."

She wrinkled her nose at him and closed her menu. "Where's your spirit of adventure? What if on Saturday night Walter Wyatt serves oysters on the half shell and pickled herring and—"

"Easy," Keir interrupted. "I'll just mimic everything you do. That's half the reason I'm taking you, remember?"

It was late when they finished dinner, partly because Jessica ordered bananas flambé for dessert and insisted Keir taste the dish.

After his first bite he sighed and said, "All right. If it'll make you happy, Jess, I promise I'll never slice a banana into a peanut butter sandwich again."

Jessica couldn't help sneaking a glance at Jonathan, who was still beside the table with the cart on which he'd prepared the flaming dessert. But he didn't even twitch. Continually repeated shocks could do that to a person, Jessica thought. Poor Jonathan was probably numb by now.

She enjoyed herself more than she'd expected, though, and when she finally pushed her coffee cup away, she was startled to realize that the restaurant was quiet, most of the tables were empty, and Jonathan was hovering at a distance with the black leather folder that contained the bill.

As Keir looked over the bill, Jessica watched him with trepidation. But he merely started peeling money off the roll in his pocket, his face almost expressionless.

"Don't worry, Keir," she said finally. "I know we'll have to keep a closer eye on the budget after this, but I thought for tonight..."

"Who's worried?" Keir's voice was light. "We're going to be millionaires. And in the meantime, we've got Bernie to fall back on."

"Good thing, too," Jessica said wryly. She reached under her chair for her handbag and spotted Trevor crossing the room from one of the most intimate small alcoves toward the door with a woman on his arm. The breadth of Trevor's body kept Jessica from seeing anything more of the woman than a floating red dress and a cloud of blond hair. But from the way the woman was clutching Trevor's arm, Jessica had no trouble identifying her as the unknown fiancée.

She wondered if the woman knew Trevor was more interested in her money than anything else. Perhaps she didn't care. Or perhaps that remark of Trevor's about wishing he could marry Jessica instead had only been another of his lines.

Keir closed the black leather folder and handed it to Jonathan. "Was that the rising executive I saw leaving just now, Jess?"

Keir could be every bit as annoyingly persistent as a small child, Jessica thought. "I wasn't paying attention."

"Well, it certainly looked like him—with a blonde on his arm. Of course, if you're patient for a bit, till we get our money, there's no reason you can't have him back."

As if I was stupid enough to still want him, Jessica thought. She tried to keep her voice casual. "I'm afraid not. He's engaged."

Keir was obviously taken aback. "Now that's amazing. Her hair looked bleached to me, and he never seemed the type to—"

"Keir, it's closing time."

He stood up lazily and held her chair. "Of course, it's not the end of the world. Engagements can be broken. But even if he doesn't come around, you won't have any trouble finding someone else."

"I don't want anyone else." Belatedly, Jessica heard the unintended meaning in her words, and she gritted her teeth for an instant in frustration. "I mean, I don't want anyone at all."

"Jess, Jess. Just because things didn't work out with him doesn't mean no other man would want you. With the kind of stake we're talking about, you should be able to snag someone with much more potential than the rising executive."

"Keir, that is *not* what I—"

Keir didn't seem to hear. "Someone who already has some money, maybe. I should think if we both put our minds to it, there won't be any trouble at all in finding someone even better suited to you, and definitely richer."

"Thank you," Jessica said with frigid courtesy, "but—"

"Oh, any time. It's my pleasure to help. Actually, I think it's just as well the rising executive went his own way, Jess. He never seemed quite right for you, somehow. Even before I knew you were a Bennington, I could see that he just didn't have your kind of class."

"Keir—"

"Yes, dear?"

She could see nothing in his eyes but sincere concern, so Jessica gave up the idea of making him understand. "Never mind."

Jonathan was in the foyer, and Keir stopped to shake his hand once more. "Thanks for the lessons, old boy," he said cheerfully. "Tell me, if this plan I'm working on at the moment doesn't come off, would you train me to be a waiter?"

Jonathan said woodenly, "Certainly, sir. You're a fast learner."

"See?" Keir appealed to Jessica. "I'm not so hopeless after all." He helped her into her coat and took her arm, handing his car keys to the parking valet. "It's the rust-colored one," he said helpfully. "Not that it was that particular shade when it came off the assembly line, you understand, but over the course of time, as it's aged into a classic..."

Definitely an original, Jessica thought. In fact, in some ways Keir bore an incredible resemblance to the few memories she had of her grandfather—the husband who had driven Clementine Bennington to distraction with his cigars and his off-color stories. Not that Jessica had been privy to the punch lines, but she would never forget the sound of his uproarious laughter.

As he drove across town, Keir whistled softly and almost tunelessly. Jessica thought he probably was unaware that he was doing it. In fact, he seemed almost

unaware of her. And though he walked her up the long
flights of stairs to her apartment, he refused coffee. "I've
got a lot of work I want to do," he said, and flicked a
finger across her cheek. "See you tomorrow, Jess."

She let herself into the apartment and turned on a
single lamp. The traffic noises that floated up from the
street only emphasized the silence inside the apartment.
The air smelled as stale as if not a molecule of oxygen
had moved all day.

Her fingertips crept to the spot he'd touched on her
cheek. Of course, she hadn't expected that he'd kiss her.
She hadn't wanted him to, for heaven's sake!

But it *would* have been nice not to have to come in
alone, and to have coffee and a bit of conversation to
look forward to instead of lonely silence.

How much things could change in a couple of days,
she thought. Just yesterday she'd been planning—un-
consciously, perhaps, but firmly nevertheless—to spend
her life with Trevor. And tonight they'd each been out
to dinner with a brand-new fiancée.

She looked at Bernie's grandmother's ring. Even in
the dim yellow light, the emerald flashed green fire and
the diamonds sparkled. She wondered what kind of ring
Trevor had bought his intended bride, and if it had meant
anything more to him than this ring meant to Keir.

She was glad, if she had to be caught in a meaningless
engagement to someone, that it was Keir. At least he had
a sense of humor. The prospect of being involved in this
scam with someone who couldn't laugh at circumstances—and at himself—was a daunting one. But of
course since this was essentially a gigantic practical joke,
a man without a sense of the ridiculous would never have
come up with the idea in the first place.

That appreciation of the absurd could be one of the
most annoying things about Keir Saunders, but it was
also one of the most attractive. That, and his smile.

Funny how she'd never noticed before how very good-looking he was when he smiled.

"And that fact," she told herself firmly, "should serve as a warning to you!"

Jessica dragged Keir away from the office the next afternoon to be measured for a tuxedo, but it wasn't an easy task.

"Do you realize what this interference is doing to my work load?" he complained as he parked the car near the shopping mall. "I *still* haven't finished debugging that damned program, and it looks as though I'll never get started on the next version."

"It'll wait," she said firmly. "You've got to have a tuxedo for Saturday night. Unless, of course, you've decided to give up the whole idea of Softek."

Keir sighed. "And have you hassling me about sales again? No, thanks. I should have taken you up on the coffee last night, you know. Not only did I not get any serious work done, but I fell asleep at the computer and had nightmares."

"About what? The size of the bill at Felicity's, or the bugs in the program?"

"Neither. I was being chased by one of your barbecued bananas." He came around the car and opened her door. "I don't see why we needed to come all the way over here, anyway. There are rental places all over town. They're a dime a dozen."

"And so's the fit they produce. Really, we should go to a tailor and have a tux especially made for you—"

Keir made a noise that sounded as if he was strangling.

"But there isn't time," Jessica went on. "Anyway I don't suppose we could justify the expense for something you'll wear once or twice."

"*Twice?* Just when, besides this party, do you expect me to put on this costume?"

"There are important occasions in a man's life when—"

"I don't understand, Jess. If these occasions are so all-fired important, why does a guy have to dress up like a penguin to take part in them?"

Jessica decided to ignore him. Though Keir's complaints were on the loud side, at least he hadn't cut and run. "To answer your question, I brought you all the way over here because even though it's a rental place, the staff takes extra care with fitting and alterations. It costs more, but the result is worth it."

Inside the shop, Keir looked around at the tuxedos, in almost every shade of the rainbow, displayed on mannequins scattered at random on what seemed an acre of plain gray carpeting. His eyebrows went up at the spectacle of a pure white suit with a matching top hat. Silver sequins sparkled on the lapels and lined the satin stripe on the trousers. "Jess—"

"Absolutely not!"

Keir's eyes started to sparkle dangerously, and Jessica regretted her tone of voice. Why had she risen to the bait? He *must* be joking—wasn't he?

He said plaintively, "But if the goal is for me to stand out, what better way—"

"Not in silver sequins, believe me."

He relented. "How do you know about this place, anyway? Do a lot of guys take you along when they shop for formal attire?"

"Not exactly."

"Oh? Does that mean you only accompany a select few? Should I be jealous? After all, since you're engaged to me now—"

"Don't waste your time pretending, Keir."

He shrugged. "I thought perhaps I should get into practice. I have so little experience of what a fiancée expects, you see, but I thought just a touch of jealousy might give an aura of realism to the whole—''

''Perhaps it would, if you could carry it off. But watching you try would certainly give me another headache, so don't do it.''

''*Another* headache? Poor darling. How *do* you know about this place?''

Jessica had thought he only concentrated so firmly where computers were concerned, but she'd obviously been wrong. No doubt before this stunt was finished she was going to find out more about how Keir Saunders's mind worked than she'd ever dreamed of wanting to know. ''A few years ago, while I was still at finishing school, I wore a tux to a formal dance. I rented it here, and it didn't fit at all badly by the time they were finished with the alterations.''

Keir took two steps back and looked her over thoughtfully. Jessica tried to ignore the appraisal—heaven knew she'd been studied by men before!—but there was something about this inspection that made her extremely nervous. It wasn't that Keir's was a sensual gaze. She didn't have the uncomfortable sensation of being stripped or touched, as she had sometimes when men looked at her. In fact, it felt more as if he was studying her with curiosity—as if she was a complex math problem he'd set about solving.

''I'd like to have seen that,'' he said.

Though the words were commonplace, there was something about his voice that sent a little shiver down Jessica's spine—but before she could assess the feeling, a salesman hurried up.

Jessica told him what they wanted, and he led them off down a row of mannequins to a fitting room. She waited outside, fidgeting with the puce satin lapel of the ugliest tux she'd ever seen in her life and listening to the indistinct murmurs of their voices—Keir's deep and rich and full of humor, the salesman's higher-pitched and ingratiating. She only hoped the man wasn't *too* obsequious, or Keir might come out wearing chartreuse instead of the basic black she'd suggested.

The shop door opened again and a young woman hurried in, glanced around and gave a sigh of relief. "Maybe I'm not late after all," she said, obviously to herself, and fluttered over to a pale cream tuxedo displayed on a child-size mannequin. She walked all the way around it, caught a glimpse of Jessica in a nearby mirror and stopped dead. "My heavens, if it isn't Jessica Bennington!"

Jessica repressed a sigh and stepped out from behind the puce tuxedo. "Hello, Sloane."

Sloane Elliot tipped her head to one side, showing off her wide-brimmed black hat to the best advantage. "Long-lost Jessica Bennington," she mused. "Darling, I haven't seen you in ages! Where have you been keeping yourself?"

"Here and there," Jessica said vaguely. There was no point in being specific. Sloane scarcely ever listened, and even if she did, she'd hardly be interested in Toolshop Software. "And you?"

"Oh, darling, it's been the most marvelous year.... I'm getting married in ten days, you know. In fact, that's why I'm here—to meet the mother of my little train-bearers, so we can get them measured again. They're identical twins, of course, and you won't believe the trouble I've had over them. They've grown so fast we've had to arrange for their tuxes three separate times. But it's worth it; they'll be perfect. They absolutely match my bridesmaids. If I'd realized you were still in town, Jessica, I'd have asked you to be a bridesmaid, too."

Sloane meant well, Jessica told herself, though she wasn't altogether sure she believed the woman. They'd known each other since finishing school days, but they'd hardly been close.

"With that dark hair you'd have fit right in with the other six I chose. Though perhaps, with everything considered ... Well, I'm sure it's more comfortable for you this way, isn't it?"

Jessica's face froze. Sloane meant, of course, that she knew perfectly well Jessica could no longer afford the expenses of being a bridesmaid in a wedding pageant like the one she was describing. Matching a pair of trainbearers to the bridesmaids and choosing the bridesmaids by their hair color—indeed!

For a moment, Jessica was almost glad her grandmother was no longer around. Witnessing that kind of slight would have given Clementine apoplexy. And for the first time, Jessica was almost as happy that there had been no Bennington inheritance. At least now she knew who her friends were. Not that she'd ever had any great illusions about Sloane.

"Nobody seems to know what happened to you," Sloane went on. "What are you doing here, anyway— besides hiding behind a mannequin?"

Before Jessica could answer, the dressing room door opened and Keir appeared. He was wearing black tuxedo trousers and socks, and nothing else.

Sloane gasped.

Jessica felt a little light-headed herself. Even though she'd cried in his arms just yesterday and realized, despite her preoccupation, how muscular he was, she'd had no idea how his body tapered, smooth and tanned, from strong, wide shoulders to narrow hips. And of course she'd never had occasion to wonder whether the hair on his chest was curly. In fact, it was a mat of dark, crisp curls that a woman could spend hours twisting and toying with—

And that, she told herself briskly, was more than enough of *that!*

"Jess," he said, "I want you to look at— Oh, sorry, darling. Who's your friend?" Sublimely unconscious of his half-naked state, he held out a hand to Sloane.

"Well," she purred. "I can certainly see why Jessica's standing around waiting for you!"

"She has to," Keir confided. "Love, honor, obey and wait for me in clothing stores—isn't that how the wedding vows go?"

Jessica wanted to groan. Why couldn't he just leave the subject alone? There was no need to tell Sloane about this masquerade.

Sloane blinked. "You're *married*?"

Jessica thought the question sounded like an accusation.

"Not yet," Keir said easily. "But the delay wasn't my idea."

It was definitely time to take a hand, Jessica thought. "Sloane, I'd like you to meet Keir Saunders, my fiancé." The word felt funny on her tongue, like the tickle of an overcarbonated soft drink. "Keir, this is Sloane Elliot, who went to school with me."

Sloane's eyes narrowed calculatingly, as if she was running through her mental social register to see if she could place the name. "Saunders?" she said. "I don't believe—"

Before the woman had a chance to say something really blighting, Jessica slid her hand through the crook of Keir's arm and tipped her head coyly against his shoulder. "And by the way, you've got those vows wrong, sweetheart," she murmured. "You're the one who has to promise to wait for *me* in stores."

Keir grinned. "As soon as we're married, I'll wait for you anytime and anywhere, beloved." He pulled her closer and dropped a kiss on her temple.

The warmth of his bare chest against her arm, the smoothness of his skin under her hand, the scent of his soap and the casual touch of his lips on her face sent the blood pounding through Jessica's body. She was suddenly so light-headed that she had to clutch at him in an effort to keep her balance.

Keir chuckled and slipped his other arm around her. "Jess," he murmured, "you're in public. What would your grandmother say, darling?"

"Oh, please." Sloane sounded disgusted. "Spare me the romantic demonstrations. I'm convinced. You must be in love, if you're actually allowing him to call you Jess. Oh, there's my friend with the twins for their fitting. It was nice to see you, Jessica."

"And when did you say your wedding is?" Keir asked smoothly.

"Ten days."

"Oh, that's a shame. Jess and I have plans for that weekend."

For a moment, Jessica thought Sloane was going to point out that she hadn't issued an invitation to either of them—but at the last minute her manners won out. "That's too bad," she purred. "I'd have looked forward to it." She hurried off toward the woman who had just come in.

"Nice people you hang out with, Bennington," Keir said, under his breath.

Jessica couldn't help seeing red, even though she knew she was being unreasonable—Sloane's behavior had been too much to overlook, and she couldn't blame Keir for his reaction. It took effort to swallow her annoyance and ask levelly, "What did you want me to look at, Keir?"

"Nothing, actually. It was just an excuse to see what was going on out here before things got out of hand."

"Well, thanks for the good intentions, Keir," she said stiffly. "But I don't need you to rescue me."

"Oh, I wasn't rescuing you, I was looking out for myself. The last thing I'd like to do is rig myself out in this suit again to watch that female hyena get married."

"Don't you mean half a suit?" Her voice was tart.

Keir looked at his attire as if to check what he was or wasn't wearing. "Jess, you sound as if it bothers you to see me like this."

"Of course it doesn't bother me," Jessica snapped. "I love watching men prancing around half-naked!"

"Really? I'll remember that." He vanished into the dressing room once more, leaving Jessica biting her tongue in frustration.

When he came out twenty minutes later he was once more wearing jeans, and the tuxedo was draped over the salesman's arm. Jessica didn't bother to ask about the fit. If something went wrong, she told herself, Keir had only himself to blame.

They were almost back to Toolshop before either of them spoke. "Jess," Keir said finally. "I'm sorry I interfered. When I heard her make that crack about you hiding out..."

Jessica looked straight ahead. "It's true, though," she said. "My friends didn't turn their backs on me so much as I pulled away."

"Because you didn't want to embarrass them?"

Jessica nodded.

There was a long silence. Keir parked the car behind Toolshop's building. Jessica was getting out of the car when he said, so quietly that she hardly heard him, "A real friend wouldn't have let you pull away."

She didn't answer, and she didn't look at him. Tears stung her eyes.

Keir seemed to understand—and that left her feeling more confused than ever.

CHAPTER FIVE

CLEMENTINE Bennington had always said that a woman, no matter what the circumstances of her life, should never be without a basic black dress. Jessica hadn't worn hers since Clementine's funeral, when she'd paired it with a herringbone tweed jacket and a black hat, but it was still hanging at the back of her closet.

On Saturday night, as she pulled the dress off the ironing board, she was almost wishing she'd taken Keir up on his offer of cash for a shopping spree. A new dress would have gone a long way toward making her feel up to the challenge they faced tonight at Walter Wyatt's Mission Hills estate.

But she knew that the kind of outfit it would take to impress someone like Walter Wyatt was well beyond their budget. No matter how free Keir was feeling with his friend Bernie's money these days, Jessica hadn't forgotten that every dime of it would eventually have to be paid back. And she wasn't nearly as certain of their success as Keir seemed to be.

Besides, simplicity was always better than showiness, and quality was always to be preferred over trendiness. With any luck, Walter Wyatt wouldn't even notice that Jessica's dress wasn't brand new. Or, if he did, perhaps he'd conclude she was merely an eccentric Bennington, not necessarily an impoverished one.

The doorbell rang just as she pulled the dress over her head. Keir was early. Jessica swore and reached hastily around to pull up the zipper, which promptly stuck at the waistline.

77

"Just a second!" she called.

It wasn't the first time she'd regretted the apartment's lack of a full-length mirror; two minutes of fiddling with a zipper she couldn't even see got her nowhere. Finally, in utter frustration, she flung the door open.

Keir was leaning against the railing at the top of the stairs, arms folded across his chest, looking completely at ease despite the severe formality of his tuxedo.

Jessica envied him his coolness. Clementine had taught her how to project an air of calm no matter what the circumstances, but in times like these she had trouble feeling serene.

Keir shifted his feet and ran a hand over his hair. "Well? What do you think?"

The small signs of nervousness made Jessica feel better—he wasn't quite as collected as he appeared. She looked him over from head to foot. His curls were more subdued than she'd ever seen them, his shoes had a mirror shine, and in between... "You look great," she said honestly. "The rental place outdid itself."

"They did, as a matter of fact." He tugged gently at his collar. "The salesman even offered to stick around late and help me with the bow tie." His gaze slid easily over her, pausing thoughtfully at the narrow strap that persisted in slipping off her right shoulder, then proceeding all the way to her stocking-clad toes. "I wish I could return the compliment, Jess. You appear to be a little—shall we say, frazzled?"

"Thanks for noticing," she said dryly, and turned around. "See what you can do with this, all right?"

"Great neckline," Keir murmured. "Shows off your shoulders wonderfully, to say nothing of—"

"Just zip the dress, Saunders."

"Maybe you should start a new style." His fingertips insinuated themselves under the edge of her dress.

"Ouch! The zipper's hot. In fact, the whole dress feels warm. What have you been doing, Jess?"

Jessica squirmed away from the ticklish touch. "Pressing out the wrinkles. Aren't you done yet?"

"I'll get it real soon now."

She shot a suspicious glance over her shoulder.

Keir grinned. "Hold still," he ordered, "or I'm apt to rip the whole back out of this thing."

She managed to stand perfectly quiet while he fiddled, but it took all the self-control she could muster. There were little prickles running from his fingertips through every cell of her body, and instead of dissipating with distance, the sensations seemed to multiply the farther they went.

But finally the zipper slid free and eased into place, and Jessica moved away from him, smoothing her hands over the narrow skirt, then stepped into her high-heeled black pumps.

Why the two extra inches of height the shoes provided should make her feel better was beyond Jessica's understanding, because the top of her head still came barely to Keir's earlobe. It was funny that she'd never felt so tiny and fragile around him before. He certainly hadn't grown taller in the last couple of days. It must be the formal clothes that suddenly made him look more imposing. Or perhaps it was the fact that she was seeing him in different surroundings. He seemed to occupy all the space in her apartment.

Not that there was much. The single room was so small that even her few possessions made it look crowded. In one corner was a pillow-heaped daybed, masquerading at the moment as a couch. Along one end wall was a tiny kitchenette, and a closet-size bath completed the apartment.

Keir was looking with what appeared to be fascinated interest at the best piece of furniture she owned, an antique ebony sideboard that had belonged to Clementine's grandmother. The top was inlaid with an intricate pattern of varicolored woods, and on the hand-carved doors were mounted two more inlaid panels, silhouettes in wood of the original owners. "That's the most incredible piece of furniture I've ever seen," he said.

"It's one of the few that survived the family crash." Jessica opened the bottom drawer beside the kitchen sink and took out a plastic dish that had once held cake frosting. She popped the lid off and tipped a strand of pearls into the palm of her hand.

"Nice necklace," Keir said. "But don't Benningtons believe in jewelry boxes?"

"People who live in cheap studio apartments with flimsy locks shouldn't believe in them, no matter what their last name is. Where do you think a burglar looks first, anyway?"

"Since I've never owned a string of pearls, it hadn't occurred to me to wonder."

"Always put your valuables in an unlikely spot. That way, there's at least a sporting chance a thief will miss them." Jessica tipped her head and fastened the pearls around her throat. "If we really get down on our luck," she said quietly, "I suppose we could pawn these. They're real."

For a moment she thought he wasn't going to answer at all. Then he said casually, "If they're valuable, why have you held onto them this long?"

She almost regretted bringing up the subject. "Because they were my mother's. They came to me on my sixteenth birthday—that's why they didn't get caught up in the great Bennington smash. The necklace is the only thing I have of hers." To her annoyance, her voice choked with emotion on the final words.

Keir put a fingertip under her chin and raised her face. "We will not be pawning your mother's pearls anytime soon," he said gently.

Jessica nodded, feeling absurdly grateful that he seemed to understand. Her fingertips caressed the smoothness of the necklace, already warm from the heat of her throat. "I guess I'm ready," she said, and reached for the coat hanging on the back of the apartment door. "This is hardly the thing for evening wear, but I suppose I can just leave it in the car. I cleaned out my wardrobe when I moved in here, since I didn't have room for a lot of clothes. And since I didn't see much need for black velvet capes and fur muffs and white satin gloves..." Her voice trailed off.

Keir didn't answer. He was looking around once more, as if appraising the apartment. His gaze came to rest on a small group of family photographs, arranged with care on an old-fashioned silk doily atop a small table in one corner.

Jessica, seeing the single room as if for the first time, sighed. The carpet was worn in spots, and the wallpaper had faded over the years. The kitchen faucet had started dripping last weekend, and the landlord hadn't fixed it yet. "The whole place looks pretty sad, doesn't it?"

Keir took the coat from her hands and helped her into it. His touch was efficient, almost brisk. "I would have said it looks brave."

Jessica looked over her shoulder at him in surprise, but before she could ask what on earth he meant, Keir took her arm, locked the door behind them and started down the stairs.

At the curb directly in front of the building, gleaming in the soft glow of the streetlights, was a white Porsche. Keir walked straight up to it and pulled a key from his pocket.

Jessica stopped dead on the sidewalk. "Where'd you get a Porsche, Keir?"

"Nice, isn't it? It's Bernie's. I told him how good you'd look in a white car, so he suggested—"

Jessica didn't move. "Your friend Bernie loaned you this car?" She had no idea what Porsches cost these days, but there was no mistaking that this one was not only almost new but from the very top of the line.

"Why not? He has a Corvette, too. It's powder blue, though—not really your color at all."

Jessica was hardly listening. "I think I should meet Bernie," she muttered.

Keir shrugged. "All right, I'll introduce you. He'd no doubt appreciate meeting you, too, especially since he's between ladies at the moment. He's not exactly the sort I'd have thought of for you, as a Bennington, but—"

"If I'd known how seriously you were going to take my heritage, Keir, I'd never have told you about it."

"What a loss that would have been for both of us!" He opened the car door with a flourish and helped her in.

As she settled herself in the leather seat, Jessica's hand touched something soft, warm and furry, and she almost screamed before she realized that the mound next to her was inanimate.

"Bernie's last girlfriend left that behind," Keir said casually. "It was just taking up space in his guest closet, and he thought you might like to use it."

The wrap was black mouton, lined in red satin. Jessica snuggled it around her shoulders. "The woman was crazy to go off and leave this."

"I understand she made a very sudden departure. I think it may have had something to do with a pot of coffee Bernie threw at her."

"A pot of— Maybe I *don't* want to meet him."

"Well, he does have his flaws," Keir said mildly. "I don't think, personally, that he's at all your type, but of course it's up to you, Jess."

The Porsche's engine started with a tiny throb and ran so quietly that Jessica was hardly aware of the vibration. She settled back to enjoy the ride and the soft warmth of mouton around her shoulders. A hint of perfume clung to the wrap. It was a pleasant scent, but very different from the one Jessica used. It was more musky and sultry, and she couldn't help but wonder about the woman who had left the wrap behind. "Did you know her?"

"Who? Bernie's girlfriend? I'm not sure—I have trouble keeping track of them. I seem to remember a redhead who might have been the one." Keir didn't sound interested. "Didn't you say the Benningtons used to live out this way?"

The miles had gone by smoothly, and Jessica was surprised to see that they were on Ward Parkway. It was a busy thoroughfare, lined with big old houses set well back from the traffic, each widely spaced from its neighbors, many with fountains or statues in courtyards that fronted on the street.

"It's still a couple of blocks away," she said. "And the front isn't actually on the parkway, it's around the corner."

"That's nicer, I'd think. Quieter, at least."

"Maybe. The house is stone, though, and the walls are about a mile thick, so I never noticed noise."

"Bet it took you a while to get used to the apartment."

"It would have if I'd moved directly there. But I was at school for years, and then I lived with Grandmother, so— There it is."

The Porsche slowed, but they were past before either of them could get more than a glimpse. Keir said, "Want to go around the block? We've got time."

"It's not necessary," she said firmly.

He flicked the Porsche's turn signal anyway. "Well, I'd like to see it better."

Jessica glanced at the house and looked away. The brief glimpse was enough to tell her that the beveled glass windows glowed like diamonds, and the tall wrought-iron gates at the end of the driveway stood open as if awaiting a returning master. The paving brick and cut stone of the irregular facade seemed to gleam in the yellow light cast by the carriage lanterns on the gate-posts. A scattering of leaves blew across the drive as the car crept past, and the rosebushes Clementine had planted under the front windows swayed in the breeze.

The house wasn't the largest on the block, but its steep slate roof and the old vines that climbed the pillars of the sun porch at one end lent it an air of solidity and permanence that bigger and showier houses often lacked.

"Nice," Keir said, as he turned the Porsche onto the parkway. "Very nice."

"Yes. At least, it used to be." Jessica's voice was stiff. "I have no way of knowing what the new owners have done with it."

He cast a curious glance at her. "Why didn't you want to see the house, Jess? Because you don't miss it at all, or because you miss it too much?"

"This persistence of yours is quite inconvenient, Keir— do you know that?"

"Usually people just call me stubborn," he pointed out. "So which is it?"

"Neither. The house is part of the past, that's all. There's no point in clutching at things that are long gone, so I hardly ever come out here."

"In other words, you miss it too much," he said softly.

Jessica gave up. "Of course I miss it, but that doesn't mean I never think of anything else. Now will you drop the subject, Keir?"

They left the parkway and swung west toward Mission Hills, the jewel of metropolitan Kansas City.

"Why did you live with your grandmother, anyway?" Keir asked a couple of minutes later.

"Because she was ill. Oh, you mean before that? My parents divorced when I was three, and my mother took me home to her parents. Then Mother died, so I stayed with my grandmother."

"Not with your father?"

"Well, I'd hardly seen him since the divorce—so I didn't exactly want to go off with a stranger when I was twelve."

Keir didn't comment. A moment later the Porsche pulled off to the side of a narrow, winding road and came to a halt behind a line of other elegant vehicles. "This is it," he said.

There was an almost breathless edge to his voice, but rather than making Jessica nervous, in a strange way it comforted her. If Keir was slightly tense, he'd be more cautious than usual—and that was all to the good.

As for me, she told herself firmly, *this is my territory.* These were the kind of people she was used to dealing with. Once inside that floodlit house, with the ice broken, she could almost put herself on autopilot.

"It's going to be dead easy," she said, as much to herself as to Keir.

He came around to help her out. Jessica put her hand in his and slid out of the car. Keir didn't step back, and she found herself blocked into a triangle formed by the car, the open door and his body. Puzzled, she glanced at him.

They were almost in darkness, except for the lights inside the car and the soft glow of the moon gleaming on his curls. She couldn't see the expression in his eyes, but she could feel a stillness about him—a kind of watchful waiting.

Then he whispered, "For luck," and bent his head.

The kiss he pressed on her mouth was as soft as a butterfly's breath. The caress didn't even smear her lipstick. Still it shook Jessica like an earthquake.

Because of the sheer unexpectedness of it, she told herself. Snatching a kiss outside the party was the last thing she'd have expected, with a whole houseful of people to impress. Keir must be even more anxious than she'd guessed.

He tucked her hand into his elbow and led her up the long driveway of Walter Wyatt's house, past the summerhouse, between the formal gardens and the pool, to the massive double front doors.

The sprawling house was modern in design, and through the enormous windows of a huge living room Jessica could see the party already in full swing. She took a deep breath as Keir rang the bell.

A butler in white tie and tails opened the door and looked them over in supercilious silence.

Keir did not attempt to shake his hand, Jessica noted with approval. Instead, he quietly gave his name.

The butler took Jessica's black mouton wrap and said, "Mr. Wyatt is receiving in the drawing room."

The room stretched the full width of the house, and it was full of people. But Jessica recognized the tycoon with no effort at all from the photograph in the magazine profile she'd studied last night. He looked older in life than in the picture, she thought. Though he was still by any description handsome, the lines in his face were deeper, his hair was more thickly salted with gray, and his body seemed softer and pudgier than it had on the magazine page.

He was standing by the fireplace, where a gas log blazed brilliantly, with a cocktail glass in his hand. A woman much younger than he, wearing a clinging fire-engine-red dress, was leaning on his arm and looking at him as if she was hanging on every word.

A trophy wife, Jessica guessed, and probably new enough in the position not to take her husband's attention for granted. She wasn't surprised, however, when the woman saw them before Walter Wyatt did. She obviously hadn't been as absorbed in his conversation as she'd appeared to be. There was cool appraisal in her eyes as she surveyed Jessica from head to foot.

She could probably guess the original value of the little black dress within a few dollars, Jessica thought, and put her chin up just a little.

With a tiny smile, the woman dismissed Jessica and turned her intense stare to Keir. Walter Wyatt said something to her, and when she didn't respond, he followed the direction of her gaze. "Are you Saunders?" he asked bluntly, and when Keir nodded, Walter Wyatt looked at the blonde and said, "Here's the man I was telling you about, Lorna. The computer genius."

The blonde held out a languid hand. "I'm charmed," she drawled. "Perhaps you'll explain it all to me."

"But not tonight," Walter Wyatt said firmly. He set his empty glass on the tray of a passing waiter. "The man's here to enjoy himself, Lorna."

"Who says he wouldn't enjoy himself?" the blonde murmured.

Walter Wyatt ignored her and turned a thousand-watt smile on Jessica. "And who's this, Saunders? I must insist on being introduced."

Jessica's fingers were suddenly firmly held between both of Walter Wyatt's big, soft hands. He loomed over her, and she caught a whiff of the Scotch he'd been drinking.

"This is my fiancée, Mr. Wyatt," Keir said easily. "Jessica Bennington."

Walter Wyatt's smile broadened. "Fiancée," he repeated. "Not wife? Careless of you, young man." His grip tightened. It was all Jessica could do not to make a face.

"Not just yet," Keir said. "But I'm only waiting for Jess to set the date. I'd marry her yesterday if I could."

He sounded perfectly earnest, but Jessica knew better than to look at him, just in case there was a telltale twinkle in his eyes. Though there probably wasn't, she concluded, since he was telling the precise truth.

"I can see why you're anxious." Walter Wyatt's gaze seemed to drink in Jessica's face. "I'm honored, Miss—" he began, and interrupted himself. "But it's silly to be so formal. I'm going to call you Jessica, because I'm sure we're going to get much better acquainted. Let me introduce you to my friends, my dear." He nodded toward the blonde. "This is my daughter Lorna."

Not a trophy wife, then. I'm out of practice, Jessica thought. She should have instantly spotted the fact that the woman wasn't wearing a ring on her left hand.

"Delighted," Lorna murmured.

Jessica tried to free her hand, but Walter Wyatt held onto it. "Lorna, don't you think these two would enjoy our picnic next weekend?"

"Why not? It's your party, Daddy. Invite everyone you like."

Walter Wyatt smiled approvingly. "That's my girl. How about it, Jessica?"

Jessica wished she dared to dart a look at Keir to get his reaction. But of course there was only one answer—they couldn't turn down a second opportunity to cement Keir's position. "It sounds lovely," she said. "We'd be delighted."

"That's great. It's at my lake house in southern Missouri—just a casual weekend, so bring your swimsuit and comfortable clothes. Lorna, you'll get them a map, won't you?'' His grip on Jessica's hand grew tighter. ''Unless you'd like to ride down with me on Friday evening, Jessica. I'd love to have you.''

An entire weekend? Jessica's throat tightened with foreboding. They couldn't possibly keep up a front for a couple of days straight. ''Oh, I *am* sorry,'' she said quickly. ''I didn't realize you meant the entire weekend. I'm afraid we have another obligation.'' She glanced at Keir, hoping he'd play along.

Instead, he frowned a little. ''An obligation?''

Jessica would have kicked him if she'd been able to move, but Walter Wyatt was still holding her hostage. ''You remember,'' she improvised. ''Your mother's expecting us.''

Keir's brow cleared. ''Oh, no, darling. The anniversary party is the *following* weekend. We're perfectly free for the picnic.''

Jessica was dumbfounded. Couldn't the man recognize a hint when he tripped over it?

''That's wonderful!'' Walter beamed. ''We'll have a lot of fun. But I mustn't monopolize you tonight just because you're a new friend.''

Jessica tried not to sigh with relief at the prospect of retrieving her hand. Now if she could just get Keir alone for two minutes and straighten him out...

''Let me introduce you to everyone.'' Walter almost dragged Jessica toward a group of people nearby and rattled off a series of names so quickly that despite Clementine's training, she would never remember them.

One of the women smiled politely and said, ''What a beautiful ring, my dear. One so seldom sees that old-fashioned cut on an emerald any more, and particularly not worn by such a young woman.''

Jessica looked at the emerald, thankful that Walter wasn't clutching her left hand. Under that sort of pressure, the ring would have cut her finger by now. "It's a family piece," she said without a tremor. It wasn't exactly a lie, she told herself, even if the family in question was Bernie's instead of Keir's.

"It was handed down to your fiancé, no doubt?" Walter Wyatt asked. "Most young women would prefer a ring of their own, I'd think, but I suppose if that's all he's got . . ." He pulled her on to the next group and laid a heavy hand on a man's shoulder. "Here's someone you should meet, Jessica—a good buddy of mine and a member of my board of directors. Fred Jackson, Jessica Bennington. Jessica came with the computer whiz I was telling you about." Walter Wyatt laughed heartily. "In fact, she's engaged to him—but only till I convince her she's wasting her time."

Jackson had turned from the group with a half-smile, but as his eyes fell on Jessica the smile faded and his eyebrows drew together.

Jessica's heart seemed to freeze in mid-beat. The last person she'd expected to meet at Walter Wyatt's party was Trevor McIntyre's boss—but what she really didn't understand was why the man seemed to recognize her. She was almost certain she'd never laid eyes on Fred Jackson before, but perhaps he'd spotted her somewhere with Trevor. Or Trevor might have mentioned her name.

In either case, Jessica felt as if she'd suddenly been handed a lighted stick of dynamite. If Fred Jackson knew she'd dated Trevor, he wasn't likely to believe in her sudden engagement. And if he was anywhere close to as ruthless as Trevor had painted him . . .

She tossed a glance over her shoulder, hoping Keir was within hearing range. But he was standing with his back to her, apparently deep in conversation with Lorna Wyatt.

Trying to explain algorithms to her satisfaction, no doubt, Jessica thought tartly. Well, he probably wouldn't be much help anyway. She'd just have to take the bull by the horns and do the best she could.

She smiled sweetly and put out her hand—the one Walter Wyatt wasn't crushing. "Are you the Fred Jackson of Union Manufacturing?"

He looked flattered and a bit less puzzled. "Why, yes. Do you know the business?"

"Only by reputation, I'm afraid. A friend of mine works for you, I believe. Trevor McIntyre."

Walter Wyatt boomed, "Do you know Trevor? Well, isn't that interesting?"

Jessica couldn't see why it should be, but to her immense relief the butler appeared at Walter Wyatt's side just then and whispered in his ear. Jessica heard something about the telephone, and a moment later the tycoon was making his excuses, and her hand was free once more.

She flexed her fingers as unobtrusively as she could and had just started to make her excuses so she could go drag Keir off for a private chat when Fred Jackson stopped a waiter, handed her a glass of champagne and said, "So you're with the computer guy. Do you really understand all that programming stuff?"

Jessica smothered a sigh. She didn't even sip the champagne. Heaven knew it was going to be difficult enough to keep her balance tonight as it was. "No—but then one doesn't need to know the principles of electricity in order to run a toaster, or to appreciate the smell and taste of the hot bagel it produces."

Fred Jackson looked a bit confused.

An arm slid around Jessica's shoulders, and gratefully she leaned against Keir's side.

"Jess takes my mind off my work," he said. "I'm sure you know how relaxing it is to be able to escape now and then from the pressures of business. I was telling her just before we left home tonight—as I was zipping up her dress, in fact—that we really ought—''

Jessica drew in a long breath and fought the urge to plant an elbow squarely in Keir's ribs. What was the man thinking? She smiled at Fred Jackson. ''Would you excuse us? Whenever Keir wants me to himself he starts telling tall tales like this, and I have to take him off where no one can hear his nonsense.''

Fred Jackson nodded dubiously.

''That,'' Jessica said between clenched teeth as they made their way toward the French doors that led to the sun porch, ''was almost the craziest thing I've ever heard!''

''About the zipper? It was true.''

''What on earth were you trying to accomplish?''

''You seemed to need rescuing.''

''You could use some lessons in how to go about it, because that wasn't it!''

''Well, you said you didn't want me to act jealous, so—''

''There are alternatives between jealousy and slander. Though actually I'm beginning to think getting married wasn't such a bad idea. If I was officially Mrs. Keir Saunders, Walter Wyatt might not be stalking me like a helpless rabbit.''

''You do seem to be the hit of the party,'' Keir mused. ''He's practically drooling over you. If attracting the boss is part of the package, I begin to see what the rising executive meant about having the right wife.''

''Somehow I don't think that's quite what Trevor had in mind. And as long as you've brought that subject up... It was Trevor's boss I was talking to, and—''

''Really? Well, speak of the devil,'' Keir said cheerfully.

Jessica looked over her shoulder. ''Trevor's *here*?''

He was standing in the doorway between the foyer and the living room, looking over the crowd as if he'd just arrived. A spotlight hit his hair, turning it almost to gold, and as Jessica watched, Lorna Wyatt strolled across the room to greet him.

Jessica clutched Keir's arm and slid through the French doors onto the sun porch.

"What are you running away from?" he asked.

"I'm not. I just don't want to meet him till I've had a chance to think. Wait a minute," she accused. "You didn't sound surprised to see him."

"I spotted him a few minutes ago."

"And you didn't tell me?"

"What was I supposed to do? Pop up to the group surrounding you and say, 'Excuse me, darling, but the man you're madly in love with just walked in'?"

Jessica didn't bother to argue the point. "What are we going to do? If he says something to cast doubt on our story, or if his boss does—"

"Look at the positive side," Keir recommended.

"There is one?"

"Of course. You aren't worried about Walter Wyatt at the moment."

Jessica gave a frustrated little shriek.

"Jess, Jess. Here I thought you could deal with anything. Obviously I'd better take a hand real soon now."

Jessica put her chin up. "And precisely what do you intend to do about this mess?"

"Well," Keir murmured, "since you've asked..."

He slid an arm around her shoulders and pulled her close with an abruptness that almost jolted Jessica's breath from her lungs. "What are you—" she gasped.

Before she could finish the question, his mouth had come down on hers firmly and possessively. It was the kiss of a man who has no reason to doubt that his caress will be welcomed, and the sheer audacity of it robbed

Jessica of the power of movement. She also lost her balance, and the instant she clutched at him for support, Keir's kiss ceased being assertive and became pure seduction. He nibbled at her lips as if he couldn't get enough of the taste of her, and he was still kissing her when, somewhere behind Jessica, Walter Wyatt spoke.

"It doesn't look to me as if she's the one who's holding back, young man," the tycoon said. Jessica thought, a little hazily, that he sounded disappointed.

Keir took one last, soft kiss and raised his head. But he didn't take his eyes off Jessica's face.

Dazed, she continued to cling to him. Her knees seemed to have gone on vacation.

Keir's voice was husky. "No, sir." He still didn't look at Walter Wyatt, but at Jessica. There was a glint in his eyes that warned her to stay quiet. "You're seeing something of a celebration, actually. Jess just told me that she's changed her mind. She wants to be married as soon as we can arrange it."

Jessica's heart stopped.

"And since I already have the license..." Keir went on softly.

"You do?" Her voice squeaked with horror. Keir's hands tightened warningly on her shoulders, and Jessica cleared her throat and tried to sound enthusiastic instead. "You do?"

"Yes," he said, and looked lovingly into her eyes. "So we won't have to wait at all."

CHAPTER SIX

"WELL, isn't that a cozy plan," Lorna Wyatt drawled. "This way you can even have a honeymoon weekend at the lake, for free. Somebody's obviously been thinking ahead." The way she looked at Jessica left no doubt about who she meant.

Jessica was still too stunned to care.

"I expect the rest of our lives will be one long honeymoon," Keir said. He smiled at Jessica and gently traced the line of her lips with the tip of his index finger.

She had to smother the urge to bite him. What had happened to Clementine's training, anyway? It wasn't supposed to be so difficult to maintain her self-control.

"Daddy," Lorna said plaintively. "Do you suppose we could all get on with the party, now that the sideshow is over?"

Walter Wyatt dragged his attention away from Jessica. "Yes, of course, honey. Everybody gather around, please." He turned toward the living room. "I have something important to say." But he sounded as if his heart wasn't in the announcement.

The crowd shifted away from the sun porch. Jessica realized abruptly that she was still in Keir's arms, pressed so tightly against his chest that the pearl studs in his formal shirt had formed indentations in her ribs. She broke away from him and pulled him off to a deserted corner. "Why the *hell* did you do that?" Her voice was no more than a harsh whisper.

"Well, you seemed to be worried about Trevor, so I thought this would head off any trouble. And you also

95

said you thought being married wasn't such a bad idea after all, so—''

''I may have said it, but I didn't exactly expect you to pop up with a license! You don't really have one, do you?''

''I'm not carrying it around with me, no. But—''

''You can't even *get* a marriage license without both people applying in person—can you?''

''I don't know if you're supposed to be able to,'' Keir said cautiously, ''but in actual fact it was dead easy.''

Jessica swore under her breath. ''You honestly weren't kidding? Whatever made you think of it, anyway?''

''It was Bernie's idea.''

''You know, I'm really beginning to dislike that guy.''

''That's too bad. I was going to ask him to be my best man.''

Jessica wasn't listening any more. ''All right, I don't suppose there's any way around it. Maybe after all it wasn't such a bad idea to get the license. We can just pretend to use it, and—''

Keir shook his head. ''No. We'd be bound to get caught, and then we'd really be in the soup.''

Reluctantly, Jessica had to admit he was right. Lorna, for one, was capable of demanding to see a certificate proving there had actually been a ceremony. For that matter, she was probably capable of demanding to be invited—

''Anyway, it's only a formality,'' Keir said. ''It's not as if we—''

Walter Wyatt's voice boomed suddenly, drowning him out. ''So I'm proud to introduce you to the young man who's going to be my son-in-law, Lorna's intended husband—Trevor McIntyre!''

Jessica's jaw dropped.

Keir put a finger under her chin and gently closed her mouth. "Darling," he chided, "what would your grandmother say if she saw you looking like that?"

"My grandmother never in her life had to deal with a situation like this one." Trevor was going to marry Lorna Wyatt? *My engagement will be announced this weekend,* he'd said over dinner just a few days ago. But finding herself at his engagement party, listening to the actual announcement—while standing beside her own supposed fiancé—was like a bad dream. "I think I need to sit down."

"Want me to fan you so you won't faint?" Keir asked.

She glared at him. "Would you be serious? Keir, that entire farce we just went through was completely unnecessary. Trevor wouldn't dare say anything about us because it would cause too many questions for him. So there's no reason—"

"What about his boss? You were plenty concerned about him, too."

"Yes, but I think I was overreacting. He may have had an idea I looked familiar, but he'll probably never give it another thought. Dammit, Keir—"

"Well, overreaction or not, it's too late now. It would be a little too much to believe that you happened to change your mind *again* about marrying me."

"You could change yours," Jessica offered hopefully.

"After everything I said about adoring you? That wouldn't make me look like the most reliable employee, would it?" He pulled her to her feet. "Now let's circulate. And look happy, darling—after all, it's only a day or two till your wedding!"

Jessica felt as if the air in the party rooms had suddenly gotten dense and heavy, and each minute seemed to stretch into an hour as she circulated through the crowd. There was an air of unreality about the whole thing, she found herself thinking as she offered her best wishes to Lorna and her congratulations to Trevor, and admired the enormous diamond that had appeared on Lorna's left hand.

Trevor looked slightly bug-eyed at the sight of Jessica, but he said nothing. Another group of well-wishers was waiting for his attention, and Jessica made her escape with relief.

"Very well done," Keir murmured as they drifted into the crowd again. "Your grandmother would have been proud."

"No, she'd have been horrified," Jessica corrected. "The mere suggestion that any Bennington could get herself into this kind of mess—"

"Oh, we'll be out of it before you know it," Keir said blithely. "A month or two, tops. Nothing to it."

They were at the dessert table a little later when Trevor appeared. He glared at Jessica and said, under his breath, "What inspired you to crash this party?"

"I'm an invited guest," she said coolly.

"And him?" He jerked a thumb at Keir.

"He's the one who brought me."

"Yeah, sure. Like he's on Walter's Christmas card list! Look, Jessica, I don't know what you were trying to prove with that circus act about marrying this clown, but if you're trying to embarrass me—"

Keir said gently, "Please don't talk to my fiancée in that tone of voice."

"I suppose you're going to give me a black eye?" Trevor taunted.

"Only if you beg for it."

Jessica looked from one of them to the other.

Trevor's voice was rough. "Just stay out of my business, all right? Both of you." He hurried away.

Keir picked up a cake server and held it over a fruit torte. "Would you like a taste of this, my dear?"

"The only thing I really want is to go home."

"Trevor will think you're running away."

"Who cares what Trevor thinks?"

Keir smiled. "All right. I'll tell Walter we've got a million details to take care of, with the wedding coming up. Shall I invite him? Maybe even ask him to be my best man?"

Jessica's hand clenched on the nearest serving spoon.

"That's chocolate mousse, Jess," Keir pointed out. "I don't think your grandmother would approve if you threw a spoonful at me." He added practically, "And neither would the tuxedo place."

She let go of the spoon, and he nodded approvingly and hurried away to find Walter Wyatt and make their excuses.

Five minutes later, Jessica sank down into the Porsche's soft leather seat and let her head droop. It was incredible how much the situation had changed in only a couple of hours. A single evening that had been intended to put them well on the road to success had instead turned into a first-class soap opera.

She groaned, and Keir looked at her with concern. "What's the matter?"

"What do you think? I don't want to get married."

"You believe I do?"

She was hardly listening. "After this fiasco, I can never have a big white wedding, you know. Once a woman's been married, no matter how briefly or how privately, she can't ever—"

"Do you mean you really want a big show?"

"How should I know what I might want? When I meet the right man I might want to throw the production of the century, with orange blossom and a long white train and a cathedral full of people—"

"Where are you going to find them all?" Keir asked unsympathetically. "Your family would fit in a shower stall and have room left over for three elephants and a Volkswagen.''

''You don't need to be sarcastic about it.''

''I'm not. Just truthful. You never struck me as the sort who'd care about big white weddings, anyway. Is that the Bennington strain coming out in you?''

She sighed. ''I suppose so.''

''I'm not so sure I like it. Besides, who would give you away? Since you don't have either a brother or an uncle to walk you down the aisle at this extravaganza you're planning—''

''I'm not planning anything at the moment,'' Jessica pointed out. ''But if I was, you know who I'd probably ask? You.''

Keir was obviously taken aback. ''Well, I'm touched by your trust, but that would be one for the books. 'The bride was given in marriage by her former husband...'''

''Exactly,'' she agreed. ''And that's why I can't ever have anything like a formal wedding. Oh, well, I'll probably never find the right man, anyway.''

''Of course you will.'' Keir's tone was bracing. ''Once we get our hands on all that lovely money, you'll have men standing in line waiting to be noticed. Just think what fun it will be trying to sort out whether they're more interested in you or the cash.''

''That's not helpful, Keir.'' Her thoughts skidded off in a new direction. ''We'll just have to get out of the weekend,'' she said. ''Going through a meaningless ceremony is idiotic enough, but trying to carry on the performance for an entire weekend—''

''Wait a minute, Jessie.'' Suddenly all Keir's good humor was gone, leaving an iron edge to his voice. ''We've come too far to back out now. Or have you forgotten what the point of this whole masquerade was in the first place?''

He was right, Jessica knew. She was stymied, stuck in the web as securely as an insect trapped by a spider. Irrationally, she struck back. "Dammit, Keir, don't call me *Jessie*! Jess is bad enough, but I will not stand for you calling me Jessie."

He looked surprised. "All right. Whatever you say."

Silence descended on the car, and they were well on the way to her apartment before Jessica said, "You know, we're going to have another problem."

"Why am I not surprised about that?" Keir murmured.

"The party tonight was one thing, but we can't accept Walter Wyatt's hospitality for an entire weekend and not entertain him in return."

"Is that the Gospel according to Bennington? You know, I've been thinking about that. Your name, I mean."

"You don't have anything better to think about? Like, for instance, how we're going to eventually get out of this mess?"

"It'll take care of itself."

"I know," Jessica said. "Real soon now. The longer I think about this whole project the dicier it sounds, Keir. Did Walter Wyatt even say a word to you tonight?"

"Of course. He said hello, and—"

"But he didn't talk about a job, or ask about the software you're writing, or discuss computers?"

"Well, it was a party. I'd expect you of all people to understand that in the middle of all those fun-loving party-goers—"

"Has it occurred to you that maybe he's just not interested after all? That this whole thing is nothing more than a pipe dream of yours? Maybe the suits told him how hopeless you are, and the party invitation was only politeness—"

"Then why did he ask us to the lake? Sooner or later, he'll get around to discussing business," Keir said airily. "He wouldn't want to look too eager."

Jessica bit her tongue. Intellectually, she accepted that a man with Walter Wyatt's business experience would be canny enough to feign an interest milder than he truly felt. Intuitively, she wasn't so certain.

"I'm sure that sometime over the weekend he'll get around to talking about it," Keir added. "Didn't you tell me that more real business gets done in social situations than in boardrooms? That's why it's so important we go."

Jessica surrendered. She was doomed to spend the weekend at Walter Wyatt's lake house. She might as well admit it.

"Anyway, about your name," Keir said. "It isn't really Bennington, is it?"

Did the man never give up? And why should her name be a subject that intrigued him? "Of course it is."

"But you told me earlier tonight that Clementine Bennington was your mother's mother. So how can you—"

"When my mother took back her maiden name after the divorce, she had mine legally changed, as well."

Keir whistled. "That's one way to tidy up. I wonder how your father felt about being just another of the loose ends."

"He came around only about once a decade," Jessica said crisply, "so I never had the chance to ask him. And since he died years ago, I'll never know."

"Do you even remember his name?"

"Of course. Bryan Marschall—with a C in the middle."

"That's unusual."

"So was he."

The Porsche pulled up in front of her apartment house. "I won't come in," Keir announced.

"You weren't invited."

"Is that the kind of manners your grandmother taught you? I was going to add that I'd love to spend the rest of the evening with you, but I've got too many things to do. I'll have to find a judge to marry us—unless you'd rather have a religious service."

"Are you joking? A fraudulent civil wedding is plenty to have on my conscience, thanks."

"It won't be fraudulent, exactly. And I suppose you'll need a wedding ring that won't collide with the emerald."

"Ask Bernie. He's probably got a collection of them."

"Oh, no," Keir said soberly. "Wedding rings are the last thing Bernie would collect. I think he's allergic to the institution of marriage—which may explain why he tossed the coffeepot at the redhead when she suggested a wedding."

"I thought you didn't know anything about that incident."

"I tried not to listen to what Bernie told me, but it's all coming back to me now."

"Well, do me a favor and don't share the details. Oh, and you might ask Bernie if we can borrow the Porsche for the weekend."

"Why? Don't you think my car would make it to southern Missouri?"

"It might be fun to see you explain to Walter Wyatt why you're driving it."

"Don't you think I could convince him that it's a classic I'm going to restore someday?"

"Keir," she said, very sincerely, "I think you could come up with a story for any occasion."

"Thanks—I think." He walked her to the front door. "I'll call you as soon as I have a time for the wedding."

"I can hardly wait," Jessica said acidly.

Even in the dimness of the streetlights, she couldn't miss the mischief in Keir's eyes. "I feel exactly the same way." His voice was theatrically husky. "So, just to hold me over till then—"

Before she could dodge or even prepare herself, Jessica was swept off her feet and into a classic Hollywood embrace. Off balance and bent over Keir's arm, she was completely defenseless. He took his time, exploring her mouth and nibbling her lips, and one of Jessica's few coherent thoughts was that she'd never before been quite so thoroughly kissed. Even on the sun porch she'd known that a good deal of Keir's attention had been focused on the crowd of party guests instead of on her.

And this kiss, she reminded herself, even though there was no audience, was every bit as much for effect. She'd never be able to look at him again without her face coloring with the memory of this embrace—and the image of a blushing bride was no doubt exactly what he'd had in mind.

He set her carefully on her feet and steadied her. "I'll be picturing you," he said softly, "sitting beside the telephone, impatient for my call."

And he was gone.

Jessica didn't hear from him again till Monday morning, but it was so early when the telephone rang that she was barely awake. "Bernie must know a judge," she said as soon as she picked it up.

"Probably several," Keir agreed. "But since all his judicial acquaintances have come about because of speeding tickets rather than mutual interests, I thought we'd rather have someone else. Who wants to get married in traffic court?"

Jessica yawned. "I can't see why that would stop you."

"At any rate, I've found a cooperative judge, and our wedding is scheduled for noon. I thought you'd like some warning, or else I wouldn't have called so early."

"Thanks a lot," Jessica muttered. "It's extremely thoughtful of you."

"I try," Keir said modestly.

"Keir, why do we have to rush into this today?"

"I suppose we could even wait till the weekend and invite both the Wyatts to be our witnesses, but—"

"No, thanks. But do I really have to give up my lunch hour for something as unimportant as marrying you?"

"Jess, darling, surely you realize I'm planning to take you out for a celebration afterward."

"That's supposed to make me enthusiastic?"

"It'll have to be a fast lunch, though. I'm determined to get this software up and running before the weekend."

"Then I won't keep you away from your work right now," Jessica said calmly, and put the telephone down.

She pushed the blankets back, padded across the small room to the kitchenette to make a cup of instant coffee, and drank it while standing at the window overlooking the empty lot behind the apartment building.

What a way to start her wedding day—and what a different picture it was than the one Jessica would have planned. Weddings weren't a subject she'd spent a great deal of time thinking about. But the realization last night that the rules of etiquette said she could never have a formal wedding once she'd gone through with this plot had reminded her of what she had once dreamed her wedding day would be.

The morning would begin with a gaggle of laughing bridesmaids, still in their nightshirts and pajamas, converging on her from the guest rooms where they had spent the night. Then a long, leisurely bath, a manicure, visits from the hairdresser and the makeup artist and the final arranging of ivory satin and lace and orange blossoms. A limousine to the church, a smile for the press cameras waiting outside...

Her eyelids stung, and she resolutely blinked the tears away and asked crossly, "How juvenile can one woman be?"

Many of those things had stopped being possibilities years ago. It was wholly unrealistic to picture the Bennington mansion when she thought of dressing for her wedding—the house had been gone for the better part of a decade.

Other bits of her dream had vanished with Clementine's death and the end of her annuity income. There was no longer money for elaborate flowers and dresses and photographs. And there wasn't an inexhaustible list of friends from whom to choose those special bridesmaids, either. How quickly, Jessica had found, the loss of the one had led to the loss of the other!

More important than those things, however, was the dream of walking down a church aisle with a heart full of love and hope and happiness, going to meet and marry the man she adored, the man to whom she was the most important thing in the world.

The shattering of that particular dream wasn't Keir's fault, of course, and she wasn't blaming him. She'd gone into this scheme with her eyes wide open.

Still, that dream was the hardest one of all to sacrifice, because she had held onto it the longest. She hadn't really begun to give it up till Trevor had so callously rejected her.

And now, because of that rejection, she was thoroughly confused. How could she have been so wrong about him? And how—having been so badly mistaken once—could she trust her judgment in the future? Could she ever again believe in what her heart said?

She dumped the dregs of her coffee down the drain and dug her pine-green suit out of the closet, then went to take a shower.

Of course there was one very good thing about her arrangement with Keir, she thought wryly. He might have dollar signs in his eyes, but at least he wasn't marrying her for the Bennington money!

Jessica had thought they might go to Felicity's again for their wedding lunch, but instead Keir took her to a small, quiet restaurant she'd never heard of before. The chintz covers on the chairs were worn and faded, the menu was very limited, and because the judge had been late and the lunch hour was past, there were only a few other patrons. No doubt, she thought, it was also much closer to their price range than Felicity's. At least, Keir obviously felt more comfortable here.

Despite what he'd said about getting back to work, he didn't seem to be in any hurry. This time he managed the wine ritual without a blunder, and Jessica inhaled the delicate aroma and nodded approvingly. ''Jonathan was right—you *are* a fast learner.''

Keir picked up his glass. ''Maybe I should have asked Jonathan to be my best man.''

Jessica could imagine the look on the maître d's face if he'd received that invitation. ''What happened to Bernie, anyway? I thought he'd be in the judge's office waiting for us. Or is he so allergic to weddings that he doesn't even go to other people's?''

''You didn't seem terribly eager to meet him. Anyway, I doubt he could have gotten away from the office today.''

Keir sounded a little preoccupied, Jessica thought. She wasn't surprised. The enormity of what they were doing had hit her like a stone at the end of the brief ceremony, after it was too late to back out. The judge had looked

intently at both of them and said a few words about the
sanctity and seriousness of the bond that had just been
created—and icicles had begun to slide down Jessica's
spine. So she could understand completely if Keir had
felt the same chill.

"What does he do, anyway?" she asked. "Bernie, I
mean."

"It's something to do with the stock market, but don't
ask me to explain it." Keir leaned back in his chair as
the waitress brought their salads. "Have you noticed how
many jobs these days are completely unexplainable?"

"Yes. Yours is one of them, as far as I'm concerned."

"Oh, that's all right. I'll provide the computer ex-
pertise, and you can contribute the savoir faire." The
humor in his voice didn't quite reach his eyes. "Is that
the word I want?"

"It'll do." The salad was wonderful, so crisp that every
bite snapped with a burst of flavor. Jessica savored a
chunk of the most enormous olive she'd ever seen and
debated what she could say to reassure him. "It's all
right, Keir," she said finally. "This whole thing isn't
permanent, you know. You said yourself it'll be over
before we know it."

"Real soon now," he agreed, but he didn't sound as
if he meant it.

"Besides, I want you to know that if Walter Wyatt
doesn't come through, I have no expectations."

"Of course you do. What's mine is yours, you know,
just as the judge said."

"Keir, be serious. We took a flyer, and if it doesn't
work out..." Jessica's voice trailed off. She wasn't quite
sure what she'd meant to say. She didn't want to sound
gloomy about their chances, and yet...

"You'll be relieved," Keir said flatly.

She thought about it as she ate the best scallops she'd
ever tasted, and finally admitted, "I suppose, in an odd

way, I would be. I've sort of gotten used to my new kind of life. It's not that I wouldn't appreciate having a nest egg, and I'd love it if I didn't have to think about whether my paycheck was adequate, but—''

"You wouldn't have to work at all," Keir pointed out.

"I'm not sure I'd like going back to having my days filled with charity tea parties and garden club shows. It's not Grandmother's fault, precisely. That kind of thing was all she knew, so it's what she prepared me for. But perhaps there's a job somewhere that would make me feel truly valuable.''

He looked as if he'd like to ask what that job might be, but before he could, a woman in a baggy yellow jumpsuit paused beside the table to eye Jessica. "Well," she said, drawing the word out into about four syllables.

Jessica smiled politely and rummaged through her memory, trying to place the features. Wild eyebrows, a strong nose, slightly crooked teeth, flyaway hair...nothing rang a bell. Surely, though, she should remember the dark eyes? Despite the undeniable curiosity in their depths, they were kindly eyes.

Maybe the woman had been part of Clementine's bridge group, or a member of her multitude of women's clubs. That would explain why she'd recognized Jessica, while Jessica didn't have a clue to her identity.

"What beautiful rings, my dear," the woman went on.

Jessica glanced at her hand. The emerald looked an even deeper shade today, reflecting as it did the dark green of her suit. And beside it nestled a quiet gold band, narrow and unostentatious, absolutely plain except for a delicately engraved edging—but obviously new.

No wonder, Jessica thought, Clementine's old friend was intrigued. There was no way to defuse that interest without an introduction. She just hoped the woman wouldn't notice that Jessica had forgotten her name.

"I'd like you to meet my husband," Jessica said politely.

Keir made a noise that might have been a stifled groan. Puzzled, Jessica glanced at him just as he pushed his chair back and stood to brush the woman's cheek with his lips. "Hello, Lydia."

The woman smiled. "So you do remember me, Keir."

"Of course."

"Well, I thought perhaps I wasn't considered a friend any more—being the last to know about your wife."

"I wouldn't exactly say that," Keir murmured. "It's all happened rather suddenly."

"Nevertheless, the next time I talk to Hannah I'm going to scold her for not letting me know. But I shouldn't interrupt what is so obviously a honeymoon." She smiled. "I'll tell Hannah how happy you both look, Keir."

"Thanks," Keir said. "It's very thoughtful of you." As soon as the woman was gone, he sat down and drained his wineglass at a gulp.

"Who's Hannah?" Jessica asked with foreboding.

"Only my mother."

"That woman is a friend of your mother's? I thought she was somebody I was supposed to recognize."

"Dammit, Jess, why did you have to tell her?"

Jessica's pride stung as sharply if she'd dipped an open wound in alcohol. Keir actually sounded ashamed of her, and the knowledge made her ache.

She snapped, "You mean you actually have a mother? And here I thought she was just something I created on the spur of the moment at the party the other night!"

Keir was silent for several seconds. "I'm sorry, Jess." He reached across the table and took her hand.

Jessica pulled away. "And don't worry about what she'll think of me," she said tightly. "I'm no more eager to meet her than she will be to meet me!"

''That's not what I meant. I just didn't want her to hear about it this way, that's all.''

''Then we'd better get back to the office, don't you think—before her friend Lydia gets to a telephone?''

Jessica didn't wait for an answer. At least, she told herself as she waited by the door for him to settle the bill, she'd never have to meet Hannah Saunders. Thank heaven this wasn't a permanent arrangement. Sooner rather than later, she'd be completely free once more. And she couldn't wait.

So why did she still feel like crying?

CHAPTER SEVEN

BY THE time they got back to the office, Jessica was already starting to feel awful about snapping at Keir. What had she expected, after all—that he'd proudly take her home and introduce her to his mother, as if this was an ordinary marriage?

In fact, she'd never given a thought to such a complication. In the months she'd worked for Toolshop, Keir had hardly even mentioned his family—and with her own solitary state, Jessica had assumed that meant he didn't have any close relatives, either.

She was bracing herself to apologize when they reached the office. But it was later than she'd thought, and Randy was already there. He was leaning back in Jessica's desk chair with his hands folded behind his neck. A slightly tinny version of a rock song was blaring from the old computer he used to copy software, and multicolored dots zinged across the screen in sync with the music.

Jessica put her hands over her ears. ''I had no idea that thing could made noise.''

Randy grinned. ''Isn't it wonderful? Of course, I could do a lot more if the speakers were better quality and the graphics were upgraded, but in the meantime—''

''In the meantime,'' Keir suggested, ''you might give Jessica her chair back.''

He was still annoyed with her, Jessica concluded. She could tell by the use of her full name. Funny—she almost missed being called Jess.

Randy jumped up so fast he nearly upset the chair. "Oh—sorry. Where have you guys been all afternoon, anyway?"

"Getting married," Keir said, and closed the door of his office behind him.

That was just like the man, Jessica thought. One minute he was upset because she'd mentioned the subject, and the next he was announcing it himself!

Of course, to be perfectly fair, there was a difference between the two situations. Randy might have to field questions from Walter Wyatt or his representatives somewhere along the line. Which was a good reminder to be careful how much she told him.

Randy's mouth was still hanging open. "He's pulling my leg, right?"

Jessica waved her left hand at him. The emerald sparkled, and the soft gold of the wedding ring gleamed.

"You mean he's not? You really did get married? Oh, man—that's just the best! I had no idea you were going to do it so soon, though, or I'd have bought you a present." He tugged at his lower lip. "Or maybe I wouldn't—I can't think of anything to give you."

"Well, don't worry about it," Jessica recommended. "There's nothing we need."

Randy looked a bit uncertain.

Jessica didn't blame him. The social nicety rang hollow in her ears, too. Under the circumstances, with Keir actually living in the office, it must look as if they needed everything.

"Now if you wouldn't mind turning the music off," she suggested, "I've got some serious work to catch up on."

She didn't accomplish much, however. Her eyes kept straying to the red light that signaled the telephone was in use. Keir was talking to his mother, no doubt—and it was taking a very long time.

When the light finally blinked off, Jessica poured a cup of coffee and tapped on the door of his office. When she went in, Keir was rubbing the back of his neck and looking as if the pressure hurt. ''Thanks, Jess.'' He took the cup and drank half the contents at a gulp.

Jessica sat down on the arm of the couch. ''How did she take it?'' she asked tentatively.

''About the way I expected.''

Which, she thought, was a singularly unhelpful description—though she wasn't altogether sure she wanted the details.

Keir took another long swallow of coffee. ''First she wanted to know what the devil Lydia was talking about. Then she choked up and asked how I could get married without inviting her—''

''Didn't you tell her it's not real?''

''I couldn't get a word in edgewise. You and my mother have certain talents in common, you know.'' There was no sarcasm in his voice, only a twinge of dry humor.

Jessica bit her lip. ''Keir, I'm sorry about telling Lydia. And I really regret snapping at you. My feelings were hurt for a minute—I guess I thought you were ashamed of me.'' She forced herself to laugh, but there was an almost hysterical note in her voice. ''If I'd stopped to think—well, I certainly wouldn't want to explain to *my* family how I'd managed to get into a pickle like this, so how can I be annoyed with you for feeling the same?''

Keir didn't answer.

Jessica resolutely hunted out a tissue and dabbed at the corners of her eyes. She didn't look at him. ''I don't blame your mother for being upset—''

His voice was rough. ''Jess, nobody could be ashamed of you.''

''Well, maybe not *ashamed*—but from her point of view I'm not exactly a prize at the moment, either. I don't have a profession, or any assets that amount to much. In fact, I've got nothing in particular to recommend me except a bloodline—and somehow I suspect my being a Bennington wouldn't carry any more weight with your mother than it did with you, at first.''

''I have to admit you're right about that,'' Keir said wryly.

Jessica crumpled up the tissue, tossed it into the wastebasket and stood up. ''I won't keep you from work any longer. I just wanted you to know I'm sorry I caused trouble.''

''Jess—''

He'd moved so quietly she hadn't realized he was right behind her, and when she turned she was practically in his arms. Keir's hand cupped her chin and turned her face to his, and Jessica felt a tightening deep inside her body, like a spring being wound too tight.

With excruciating slowness, Keir drew her closer till she was pressed against his chest. She could hear the pounding of blood in her ears, and she could feel the slow, steady thump of his heart against her breasts. She was just drawing breath for a protest when he kissed her, and the firm gentleness of his lips against hers smothered not only the words but the thought behind them. Suddenly her head was swimming. The room seemed to shudder, and she clung to him for protection.

''Oops,'' Randy said from the door. ''Sorry, guys. I finished all my work, so I thought I should tell you before I went home. Don't let me interrupt you.'' He sounded stricken. ''Tell you what, I'll lock up as I leave.'' He vanished, and only moments later the front door banged.

The room was still swaying, but Jessica managed to steady herself and pull away. ''Just what we need.'' She almost managed a laugh. ''Randy catching us acting silly.''

Keir's arm slipped slowly from around her shoulders. His voice was low. "Consider it practice for the weekend."

The tension inside her subsided slightly, though the way he was watching her—like a cat studying his prey— still made her feel a little shivery. "Is it so late?" she asked. "If it's already time to lock the office—"

"It isn't. Randy was just doing us a favor."

"Oh." Absentmindedly, she rubbed her arms, warding off a chill she was almost too numb to feel. "If you don't mind, I think I'll go home anyway. This has been sort of a difficult day." Now that line, Jessica thought, could win a prize as stupid understatement of the year!

"It has, hasn't it?" Keir said soberly. "I'll see you tomorrow."

Before she was even out of the office he'd turned to the computer.

The machine was not only his profession, she thought, but his relaxation. Sometimes Jessica envied him, wishing she had a similar kind of retreat—a sort of private refuge where she could concentrate on something purely logical and close out all the emotional nuances of the world.

It wasn't any surprise that Keir had escaped into his programming. And it shouldn't be any surprise, either, that Jessica was going home to an empty studio apartment on her wedding night.

Of course, she wouldn't have wanted it any other way.

To Jessica's relief, when she reached Toolshop on Friday morning the Porsche was parked behind the building, and Keir was in the main office washing coffee mugs.

"I see we have transportation for the weekend," she said.

He reached for a towel. "Bernie thinks I've gone completely nuts."

"Getting married?"

Keir nodded and said airily, "He seems to think you'll end up deciding to keep me."

"Well, give him a message from me—he doesn't need to worry."

"I already have. I told him as far as you're concerned, I'm just filling your time till the right rich guy shows up. I also told him that if we didn't keep up appearances in the meantime, he'd never see a penny of his money again, so—"

"Oh, that must have been a great comfort for him."

"He grew very thoughtful and said agreeably that he didn't need the Porsche this weekend, so we could take it." The coffee maker sighed as it finished the cycle, and Keir filled two mugs. "I think we should leave right after lunch. It's a good four hours down to the lake."

"I can't wait," Jessica muttered.

Keir grinned and dropped a casual kiss on her nose. "Neither can I. It *is* our honeymoon, after all." Whistling, he took his coffee into his office.

Shortly after noon, they locked up the office and he drove her to her apartment to pick up her weekend case.

"I wish I knew a little more about what Walter Wyatt means by a picnic." Jessica folded the last few items into a monogrammed leather bag that was a leftover from her college days. It was a bit scratched and worn, but still serviceable. "I've been to a few so-called casual events where mink and diamonds were the order of the day."

Keir shrugged. "Well, since you don't have either, I wouldn't worry about it."

"You're a lot of help."

"I aim to please." He looked thoughtful, and added, "Though maybe Bernie's right, and I should be more careful about being so agreeable. If that rich guy doesn't show up, you might change your mind and try to hang onto me after all.''

''I'd rather try to capture water in a sieve, Keir.'' She closed the suitcase. ''That will have to do it, I'm afraid. They'll just have to take me as I am.''

''Did you remember to put in a swimsuit?''

''Don't you think the lake will be too chilly for swimming?''

''Probably, but if there's a formal dinner party, you could wear it—with your pearls, of course—and nobody would say anything about the missing mink and diamonds.'' Keir put her luggage in the trunk beside his battered duffel bag and helped her into the car. ''At any rate, think positive—at least when we entertain the Wyatts we can arrange things on our own terms.''

''What?''

''Didn't you say we'd have to return the invitation sometime?''

''Of course, but I thought you hadn't heard me.''

''I listen to all your concerns, sweetheart.''

''Oh, really? When I first brought it up, you kept changing the subject. And you haven't said anything about it all week.''

Keir shrugged. ''I was busy with other stuff. Besides, I didn't have anything to say.''

''I'm not surprised about that, so I suppose I should take advantage of the fact that you're willing to discuss it now.''

''Jess—''

She plunged on without giving him a chance to dodge the subject once more. ''I think the minimum we can get by with is a dinner invitation. Ideally, it would be a private party—entertaining at home is a far better way to impress the boss. But I suppose we'll just have to take them to a restaurant.''

''If you're talking about Felicity's—''

''It's probably the best we can do under the circumstances.'' She nibbled her thumbnail and brightened. ''Maybe we can convince the Wyatts that we're remodeling and can't have a party at home.''

''Well, I don't suppose your apartment would be quite the thing.''

''Hardly. And since you don't even have one any more...''

''It was shortsighted of me to give it up, wasn't it?''

''Actually, it's probably all to the good. Did you even own a plate that wasn't made of paper?''

''I don't recall seeing one.''

''That leaves Felicity's,'' Jessica said. ''It's the only way out.''

''No, it's not. All this effort is admirable but unnecessary, Jess, because I borrowed an apartment we can use.''

''Borrowed... Now why didn't I think of that? Bernie's place, no doubt?''

''Oh, no,'' Keir said bluntly. ''You wouldn't like Bernie's wallpaper, and he'd be really upset with both of us if you stripped it off just for one little dinner party.''

''Then who? The real estate guy? You're doing that programming for him at a bargain rate, and he must know of a dozen empty apartments, but—''

''But we'd have to furnish it,'' Keir finished. ''Besides, I'm two weeks behind on his project.''

''That is a problem. It's certainly no time to be asking for favors.''

''I thought that's what you'd say. And I didn't think you'd want to explain to the friendly soul we ran into in the tuxedo shop that we needed to borrow her house for an evening, either.''

''Sloane Elliot?'' Jessica shuddered at the thought. ''No, I wouldn't like that at all.''

"But Bernie's sister is away on a business trip, so we can use her apartment."

"Keir, you're incredible!" It was silly, perhaps, to be so relieved over a simple dinner party, when she'd been involved in a hundred over the years, but if Keir hadn't been driving, she might have thrown her arms around him. Though maybe she should wait to celebrate till she'd seen the place.

"Bernie's got a key," Keir said, "so as soon as we get back on Sunday afternoon we can move in."

Jessica was silent for a long moment. "*Move in?* Don't you mean, stop by to see if it'll work and what we'll need?"

Keir shook his head. "House-sitting is part of the deal. In fact, Bernie said Carole seemed pleased the place won't be empty while she's gone."

"All right—but making it look occupied won't take both of us, surely."

"Jess," he pointed out gently, "have you never realized that it is accepted behavior for people who are married to each other to live under the same roof?"

"If they're really married, yes. But—"

"Or if they want others to think they're really married."

Jessica paused for a moment, then tried again. "But it's not like we have separate places, actually. Between us, we have my apartment and the business—and nobody needs to know you're spending all your time in your office."

"So far, so good. But how do you fit Carole's apartment in there?"

Jessica bit her bottom lip. "Well, my studio isn't big enough for two."

"Very true—but that argument won't exactly be convincing if you don't move. Besides, if we're going to entertain, we'll have to look as if we know where the china is."

"And we're going to lie to Walter Wyatt about it being our apartment?"

"It's not lying to say we've borrowed the place from a friend till we find something we like. But what better way to make things appear natural than to live there for a couple of weeks?"

She couldn't pick flaws in his logic, and the inability annoyed her. "Only two weeks?" she asked finally.

"Carole's on a business trip, not a sabbatical. But if you'd like renewal options, Jess, I'm sure we could arrange something."

"Of course I don't want renewal options!" She saw his eyebrows quirk with curiosity and moderated her voice. "Besides, Bernie wouldn't approve of our arrangement going on for too long."

"Oh, yes, I'd forgotten that. It's agreed, then—we'll live together for two weeks."

"Share a roof," Jessica corrected.

"But darling, what did you think I meant?"

Of course he didn't mean anything more than that, she reminded herself. She was really getting to be far too sensitive. Keir didn't want to live with her any more than she wanted to live with him.

Jessica had expected that Walter Wyatt's lake house would be far grander than the modest cabin he'd made it sound like, but she hadn't anticipated that it would be almost as large as his Mission Hills mansion. By the time Keir parked the Porsche by the carriage house, Jessica had given up on estimating the number of rooms and settled for counting wings.

Keir folded his hands on the steering wheel and peered at the house. "I've seen hospitals that are smaller."

"But none that have such a distinctive architectural style, I'll bet."

Keir stared at her, looking stunned. "Are you serious?"

"I didn't say it was *good*," Jessica reminded him. "Just *distinctive*."

Keir relaxed. "For a minute there you had me worried."

Even the massive scale of the building couldn't ruin the setting, however. Down an easy slope from the house lay the gentle curve of the lakeshore, where waves broke softly against the sand in a steady, rhythmic pattern. What a wonderful lullaby that would be, Jessica thought.

"There is one nice thing about it," Keir mused. "With all this room, Walter Wyatt can't keep an eye on us every minute. We might even be able to relax a little and enjoy the weekend."

Jessica wasn't quite so confident as Keir sounded, but she could feel some of the tension seep out of her muscles.

The same stiff-necked butler who had greeted them at Lorna Wyatt's engagement party opened the door. He was wearing khaki trousers and a matching short-sleeved shirt, and Jessica thought he looked far less comfortable in the safarilike garb than he had in white tie and tails.

"Shall I take those, Mrs. Saunders?" he asked with an air of disdain, and relieved Jessica of the bundle of flowers they'd stopped to buy in the nearest little town.

It was the first time Jessica had heard herself referred to by her new title, and she found it a bit of a jolt. As long as she was here, there would be no pretending that little ceremony in the judge's office hadn't happened.

"Mr. Wyatt is on the terrace having cocktails," the butler went on. "He asked that you join him as soon as you've freshened up, so I'll show you upstairs right now. One of the boys will bring up your bags immediately."

Without waiting for an answer, he handed the flowers to a maid, turned toward the stairs and began to climb at a majestic pace.

In the upper hall, Jessica heard footsteps, and a moment later Lorna Wyatt came around a corner wearing a strapless red swimsuit under a long terry wrap. "Thank you, Benson," she said. "I'll show our guests to their room."

The butler nodded and retreated toward the stairs, and Lorna led the way down a broad hall.

"We've got a houseful of people this weekend for the picnic tomorrow," she said. "But I shifted things around to give you what Daddy always calls the bridal suite. I hope you'll be comfortable here."

Lorna flung open a set of arched double doors to reveal a room done entirely in white. The bedspread was quilted cotton, and the pillow shams were embroidered eyelet. A drift of lace covered the high-arched canopy above the bed. Two chairs were covered with loose, cool-looking linen slipcovers. French doors stood open to a balcony overlooking the lake. It was a good deal warmer here than it had been in Kansas City, and the breeze that teased at the sheer curtains was refreshing.

"I'll leave you to get settled," Lorna said. "Do make yourselves completely at home."

Jessica wondered if she was imagining the ironic edge in Lorna's voice. She must be hearing things, she told herself. The woman didn't have any reason for envy. Lorna was engaged to a man she presumably cared for— and Jessica was morally certain Trevor had never told his fiancée about other women in his life. Unless he had, Lorna would have no reason to focus on Jessica any more than on the other women at the party that night.

Of course, it was possible that Lorna's antennae had picked up the exchange between Trevor and Jessica and Keir at the dessert table on the night of her engagement party. But Jessica was reasonably certain Lorna couldn't have seen that.

The only other possibility she could think of was that Lorna had her eye on Keir—and that was so far out of the question as to be laughable. Certainly she'd noticed him the moment he'd come into the party that night, but so had every other woman in the room. Keir was tall, good-looking and—to the women in Lorna Wyatt's crowd—slightly mysterious. Add a perfectly fitting tuxedo, and the man was nothing if not attention-getting.

But if Lorna was envious of Jessica because she had Keir, the woman was a champion example of a dog in the manger. No, Jessica decided, she must have been imagining things.

She looked around the room once more and sighed. She'd expected that the weekend would present difficulties, but she'd convinced herself that in a house this size, sharing a room wouldn't be one of them.

Obviously, she thought, not everyone had Clementine's view of appropriate guest behavior. As best Jessica could recall, every guest room in the Bennington mansion had held twin beds. Here there was only one, and there wasn't even a couch to serve as a substitute. At least the bed was king-size—that was a blessing.

"They couldn't spare two rooms?" she muttered. "How many people does it take to fill this house, anyway?"

Keir had already finished unpacking. He dropped his empty duffel bag on the closet floor and shut the door. "Why waste two rooms on a honeymooning couple?" he said reasonably, and pulled a coin from his pocket. "Want to flip? Winner gets first choice of sides of the bed."

The cocktail party on the terrace the butler had referred to had obviously been going on for some time when Jessica and Keir came downstairs. Walter Wyatt was gesturing with his martini glass, and he didn't seem to notice when his drink slopped over his arm and the paving bricks under his chair. He rose when he saw Jessica and bellowed a greeting across the width of the terrace.

She thought for a moment he was going to hug her, but she extended her hands, keeping her elbows stiff, and managed to hold him off.

"That was smooth," Keir murmured as Walter turned his back for a moment to call for the butler. "It's probably wise not to let him get too close too soon."

Jessica was stunned. What did he mean, *too soon*? But there was no time for discussion. Walter pressed drinks on them and took them around the terrace for introductions.

Lorna hadn't been exaggerating the size of the crowd. If all these people were staying at the house, Jessica calculated, they must be doubled up in all the rooms.

Lorna was lounging languidly on a long recliner beside a sparkling, steaming whirlpool, with her terry robe open to let her soak up the weak rays of the October sun. "Benson told me you brought flowers. How thoughtful." Her tone implied that she was anything but impressed.

Jessica refused to be intimidated. She smiled sweetly and moved on to the next group of deck chairs.

This time, Trevor's boss didn't show any signs of puzzlement. Jessica wasn't quite sure if she should be relieved or worried. Perhaps Fred Jackson had given up the question—but he might equally well have asked Trevor for an explanation.

He rose politely, shook her hand and introduced her to his wife. Maddy Jackson gushed, "Oh, you're the Bennington girl! My dear, I'd love to see your house. Ever since we came to Kansas City, I've wanted to know what it was like on the inside."

"Maddy," her husband said quietly.

"Oh—am I saying something I shouldn't, Fred?" She looked confused, then turned bright scarlet. "I wasn't hinting for an invitation, Miss Bennington. I only meant—"

Lorna Wyatt put a hand to her face in a halfhearted attempt to hide a smile.

Her rudeness annoyed Jessica and sent a surge of sympathy through her for the hapless Maddy. "I only wish I could invite you to see it, Mrs. Jackson, but I'm afraid the house isn't in the family any more."

"What a shame," Lorna drawled.

"It was far too big for one person," Keir added. "Now things are a little different, of course, so I'm investigating the possibility of buying it back."

Jessica kept smiling, but it took effort. "I can't wait to have a walk by the lake, darling," she said and slipped her hand into the bend of Keir's arm. "Come with me, please?"

The terrace was multilevel, with steps leading in easy stages almost to the lakeshore. From this side the house looked even more enormous. It would have resembled a fortress looming over the water if it hadn't been for the large windows.

As soon as they were out of earshot, Jessica turned to face him, put both hands on his chest in what she hoped would look from the terrace like an intimate, loving pose and said, "That was one of the craziest lines I've ever heard. What do you mean, you're thinking of buying the house back?"

Keir shrugged and slid both arms around her shoulders. The breeze ruffled his hair, and a stray beam of late afternoon sun shot gold highlights through the dark strands. "It wiped the smile off Lorna's face, didn't it?"

"Temporarily, maybe. But you shouldn't have put us out on a limb like that. It's far too easy to check whether the house is for sale, and then what?"

Keir shook his head. "I didn't say it was actually listed, and I didn't exactly invite Mrs. Jackson to come and visit us as soon as we close the deal. All I really said was that I was checking on it. One phone call to the owner to ask if it's for sale, and I've done every last thing I said I would."

"And what if it *is* on the market?" Jessica challenged. "You'll look pretty foolish then."

"So what are the odds against that happening? A hundred to one? There certainly wasn't a realtor's sign in front last weekend."

"There often aren't, in that neighborhood. But everything's for sale, at a price."

Keir shrugged. "So maybe the price is too high. Or maybe they've ruined the house and you end up deciding you want something else anyway. Besides, that kind of a deal takes time to put together, Jess. We'll be off the hook long before we could get a mortgage."

"Considering the trouble we'd have borrowing money from anyone but Bernie, that's not saying much," she muttered. "Keir, if you don't keep these crazy impulses of yours under control, you're going to land us in a whole lot of hot water one of these days."

"But you must admit that the whole concept of buying the Bennington house gives us an air of success." He tightened his grip, pulling her neatly against his chest. "And speaking of things like leaving the right impression... Since we're not out of sight of the terrace, do you suppose you could at least smile at me for Walter's benefit? He's no doubt keeping an eye on us."

Jessica obediently faked a grin, but as she looked at him her breath caught in her throat and her smile froze. Keir's eyes were a shade darker blue than the lake, and his gaze was just as enticing. It would be possible to drown in his eyes....

"You look just a bit like a tiger with a toothache," he suggested, and his hands slid slowly down her back to cup her hips and nestle her even closer against him. "If we're finished with this discussion, Jess..."

His voice was little more than a sensual murmur, as hypnotic as the slow ripple of waves across the water, and for an instant she let herself be carried away. There couldn't be any harm in kissing him. It was all in a good cause, after all.

Then, with an effort, she pulled herself together. "You might be finished, but I'm not. As long as we're talking about Walter, what on earth did you mean about letting him get too close to me too soon?"

"Well, he's the richest guy you're likely to run into anytime in the near future. But he's a pretty savvy sort, so I thought it would be wise to play him like a fish."

Jessica gasped. She might have kicked him if he hadn't had such a good grip.

"You know," Keir added helpfully, "not let him know too soon that you're trying to snag him."

"You have the gall to think I might actually be interested in *him*?"

"Lorna does. Didn't you see the way she was looking at you?"

Now that was food for thought. Jessica bit her bottom lip and considered. Keir might be right, she realized. She hadn't considered the possibility that Lorna might be jealous for her father's sake. The idea was too bizarre to have crossed her mind. "Well, just to get the record straight, I have no romantic interest in Walter Wyatt."

"Oh, I didn't say anything about romance."

Jessica was taken aback anew. "I suppose you think if I encourage him, it'll help your chances of getting the deal you want?"

Keir shrugged. "I don't have a clue. You're the one with all the experience on how this social level operates—not me. Play it however you like, Jess. Just let me know what the rules are."

CHAPTER EIGHT

TOO annoyed to worry about whether or not anyone was watching from the house, Jessica strode off down the lakeshore leaving Keir behind—and she didn't speak to him again till well after dinner. The slight didn't seem to bother him, however. He was obviously enjoying himself throughout the beef Stroganoff by explaining the history of computers to Maddy Jackson.

Jessica found herself seated next to Walter Wyatt, politely listening to how he'd built up his manufacturing empire from the single small plant his father had established and wishing that dinner-party etiquette wasn't quite so rigid on the question of who could and couldn't sit together. She'd much rather have heard about computers.

It didn't help that Lorna Wyatt was obviously giving only a halfhearted ear to Fred Jackson. She seemed to be devoting most of her energy instead to watching Jessica and her father.

Keir had been right, Jessica realized—Lorna did think that Jessica was a threat to her own position. She felt like shaking the girl. No matter what Lorna suspected, it wasn't very smart to ignore her fiancé's boss. Trevor seemed to feel the same, Jessica observed. He was sending glowering looks at his intended bride.

But finally dinner was over, and the group adjourned to play bridge. Keir, with an easy smile, declared that since the only sort he was good at was the computer version, they wouldn't want him, and he went off for a walk. Jessica bit her tongue and reminded herself that

her part of the deal was, as Keir had put it, to supply
the savoir faire for both of them. She couldn't do that
by shrieking at him like a fishwife, however satisfying
it might be.

The end of the evening didn't bring any relief, either.
Keir, back from his walk, settled on the arm of Jessica's
chair for what he termed a lesson in championship bridge
and began toying with her hair as she tried to concentrate on the hand. Distracted, she promptly revoked, and
Lorna said irritably, "If you're going to behave that way,
Keir, why don't you just take her off to bed?"

Walter looked shocked, and even Maddy Jackson
sputtered a little. Keir laughed and pulled Jessica to her
feet. "Polite guests always do what their hostess re-
quests, Jess. Good night, everybody."

On the stairs, Jessica muttered, "Now's a fine time
to learn manners—if that's what you call it."

"Admit it, Jess, you were getting tired of bridge, and
of Lorna, and even of Walter's adoring stare."

"That doesn't mean... Oh, never mind."

She seized her still-packed weekend case and shut
herself in the bathroom. She cleaned her teeth till it was
a wonder there was any enamel left, and brushed her
hair till it gleamed and her arm ached from the repetitive
motion. She cold-creamed not only her face but her
throat, hands, elbows, knees, heels and every single toe.

But she couldn't put off the inevitable any longer. She
had to come out of the bathroom eventually.

She eyed herself in the mirror and made a face. At
least she'd had enough sense to pack pajamas instead
of tossing a negligee into her bag. But her choice didn't
seem as innocuous now as it had in her apartment. She'd
have been far more comfortable in red and green plaid
flannel than she was in lavender satin trimmed with
eggshell lace.

The bedroom was quiet when she tiptoed out. The only light came from a reading lamp above the bed, turned to the dimmest setting. The quilted spread was folded neatly on the bench at the foot of the bed, and Keir was lying on his side with his eyes closed, the sheet pulled over his shoulder.

Jessica almost laughed at herself. Had she really expected he'd be watching the bathroom door like a bridegroom in the movies, waiting eagerly for her to emerge?

You're an idiot, she told herself. Just a couple of hours ago he'd practically told her to go after Walter Wyatt!

She eased into bed, turned on her back and let out a smothered yelp as she got her first look at the full-length mirror concealed in the canopy. The reflection showed the dim light from the reading lamp spilling a romantic pool of gold across the white satin sheets and the two figures within.

"What's the matter?" Keir asked.

Jessica shot a look at him, but his eyes were closed, his lashes heavy on his cheeks. "Nothing." She turned the reading light off and lay perfectly still with her back to him. It was silly to suspect, in the dark room, that she was being watched. It was even sillier to feel that the mattress sloped and if she didn't hang onto the edge she was apt to slide across the slick satin sheets and straight into Keir's arms.

And it was silliest of all to think that Keir's soft, steady breathing—which in fact was almost too gentle to hear—was vibrating the bed.

That's nonsense, she told herself. She was imagining it. The sensible thing to do was to think pleasant thoughts and drift off to sleep just as Keir had.

"Comfortable?" he asked.

She jumped, startled, and the satin-covered pillow shot out from under her head and hit him in the face.

"Sorry." She retrieved it and tried to wedge it against the headboard. "I wish you'd stop that."

"What? Talking to you? Are you sure you don't want this side instead?"

"I'm sure. You lost the coin toss, so I chose. You made the rule so you'll have to live by it." She added, warily, "Why do you ask?"

"I just thought I should warn you that I'm in the habit of sleeping on that side."

"Keir, you're in the habit of sleeping on a couch!"

"I mean, when I have a bed I always use that side. So if during the night I forget where I am and drift in your direction . . ."

"I'll put an elbow firmly in your ribs," Jessica warned.

"That will probably do the trick." His voice was as slow and lazy as cold maple syrup spreading across a warm waffle. He sounded utterly relaxed, and as silence fell once more on the room, Jessica found herself timing each long, even breath he took.

Her body felt as if she'd been hooked up to a mild electrical current, leaving every nerve twitching to a different rhythm. Her muscles ached with the effort it took to remain still—but if she moved, the combination of satin pajamas and satin sheets threatened to shoot her across the mattress in the same path her pillow had taken.

She turned her head just enough to see the digital clock on the bedside table. In the darkened room, the red lights that formed the time seemed as bright as a beacon. She watched as the numerals silently marked the passing of a minute, and then another. At this rate, she thought, the night would be several years long.

Keir was motionless, lying on his back with one arm flung up over his head, his hand loosely cupped as if waiting for someone else's fingers to be laid in his.

Jessica almost punched her pillow in frustration, envious of the rest he was enjoying. It was obvious that sharing a bed with her was no big thrill—or concern—to him.

She pushed the sheet back, moving slowly so she wouldn't disturb him, and was almost to the door when he spoke.

"What's the matter, Jess?"

She spun around. Her eyes had adjusted to the dimness, and she could see—almost too well for her own comfort—that the sheet had slipped to his waist as he sat up, leaving his chest bare.

"I can't seem to get comfortable," she said.

"Is the mirror bothering you? Or are you just not used to sharing a bed?"

"Is it any of your business?"

He didn't answer that, only ran a hand through his hair, leaving the dark curls more tousled than ever. "Where are you going, anyway?"

"To look for a book."

"At this hour? In this house? You're joking."

"When we went down for dinner I saw some shelves in the den. There must be something fit to read."

"You can't, Jess."

"Why on earth not? You don't think there are guard dogs prowling around, do you?"

"What would Walter think if he found you poking around for a book? You're supposed to be on your honeymoon."

"Oh," Jessica said. "I hadn't thought of that. Well, sometimes people can't sleep, even on honeymoons."

"But they usually don't need a book for entertainment." Keir reached up to turn on the lamp.

The movement warned Jessica, but still the sudden light seemed as brilliant as the sun, and she flung her hands up to protect her eyes. "What are you doing?" she asked suspiciously as Keir slid out of bed.

"Finding you something to read. Since this house is as big as the average hotel, perhaps the perfect butler has left a guidebook in every room. I think I saw something in one of these drawers when I was unpacking."

She tried not to watch him, but she couldn't help seeing that his pajamas were made of a blue and white ticking stripe that made him look even taller, and that they rode low on narrow hips as he leaned over to open the bottom bureau drawer.

A moment later he straightened, brandishing a paperback book. "Not a guidebook, after all. Perhaps a previous guest left it behind. It might not be your first choice of literature—"

"*The Twelve Days of Murder*?" Jessica said doubtfully. "I hardly think so."

"But then I suspect Walter's library wouldn't be quite to your taste, either." Keir handed her the book and climbed into bed.

Jessica eyed the garish cover, which featured a trench-coated tough embracing a scantily clad blonde. "Walter's books could hardly be less in my style than this is."

"Good. It'll bore you to sleep in no time at all." His voice was muffled by the pillow—he'd buried his face in it.

"I don't want to keep you awake," she said tentatively. "Perhaps if I sit on the balcony—"

"And freeze? Don't worry about me. I don't expect to get much sleep, but it won't be your reading light that keeps me awake."

Jessica felt a little better. It helped just to know that this awkward situation was bothering him, after all. She twisted the reading lamp around to a better angle, piled up the extra pillows and settled down with the book.

Either it was better than most of its genre or she was even more desperate than she'd realized, for within the first dozen pages she became interested in the story. It was almost an hour later that she realized she was shivering, and she wasn't quite sure if it was because of the cool breeze through the half-open French doors or the spooky plot. Half-afraid of her own shadow, she drew the sheet closer around her shoulders and turned the page.

Keir had gone to sleep. She was sure of it this time, because he was snoring ever so slightly. As she watched his mirror image, he rubbed his nose, flung out a hand and rolled a little closer to her. She could feel heat radiating from his body.

He must have been creeping closer for some time, she thought. She should push him away, even elbow him as she'd promised to do. But it was rather nice to have the comfort of a big, strong body nearby—even an unconscious one. She'd just close her eyes for a minute and enjoy his warmth, and then she'd get up and close the French doors and put the quilted spread on the bed....

Or maybe she wouldn't. In the unfamiliar house, with the night noises magnified by the quiet outdoors and the suspenseful book, she'd just as soon not move.

And Keir would never know the difference, anyway.

Sunlight was streaming through the French doors when Jessica woke. She struggled out of sleep, half-confused about her surroundings. She'd had a dream—the details were foggy, but she rather thought she'd been a kitten. She vaguely remembered lying on a satin pillow and being petted.

She shook her head in confusion and looked around. It was no wonder she was feeling a bit dopey, she supposed. She must have read half the night away. At that, she didn't remember turning off the light or putting her book aside, but she must have done so, for the paperback lay on the nightstand with a silk flower as a marker.

She looked from the book to the basket that held the flower arrangement. She was certain she hadn't walked across the room to pluck a daisy to mark her page. She couldn't have forgotten that. Which meant that Keir must have done so.

She turned onto her back and looked into the mirror. Keir's half of the king-size bed was empty, but his pillow remained almost squarely in the middle of the bed, and Jessica's head was on it. If he'd been using it, too, the scene must have been as sweet and intimate as anyone could have wished.

She growled a little at the thought. Then, philosophically, she snuggled into the soft quilted spread—it had been considerate of him to tuck her in—and tried to recapture her dream. In her sleep, she'd felt warm and safe and contented.

Instead of suspicious, which was what she felt now. What if she hadn't been dreaming that slow, sensuous stroking?

That didn't bear thinking about. She slid out of bed, stepping on her pillow as she did so. No wonder she'd ended up using his, since hers was on the carpet!

A long, hot shower helped to restore her equilibrium. Then she dressed in white shorts and a royal blue sleeveless top and went downstairs in search of Keir. Not that she exactly wanted to see him, she told herself, but it was better than being alone with her thoughts.

He and Trevor were sitting in the dining room, on opposite sides of the table, and Walter Wyatt was just rising from his place at the head. Jessica hesitated on the threshold.

Walter said, "Good morning, my dear. You must have read my mind—you look all ready for tennis. I thought perhaps we could organize a doubles match after breakfast."

Jessica nodded. "I'd like that."

Walter smiled approvingly. "I'd join you for coffee but I'm afraid business calls. I'll finish as soon as I can, though, now that I'm looking forward to tennis."

Keir rose to hold the chair beside his own for her. Jessica saw a glint in his eyes and braced herself.

"Hello," he said huskily, in a tone just loud enough to be certain both Walter and Trevor could hear. "I hope you slept well—when you finally went to sleep, that is."

He was referring to her book, of course. Though... Jessica felt warm color wash over her cheeks. Had she really huddled up against him for protection in the night? And if so, what ideas was Keir cherishing this morning?

Don't be a fool, she told herself abruptly. She knew perfectly well that he was only interested in creating the illusion of a loving couple, and the gleam in his eyes—which only she could see, after all—was no more than teasing.

Trevor snorted. "You certainly had me fooled, Jessica."

He pushed his plate aside and strode out.

Keir laughed softly, poured Jessica's coffee and filled his own cup.

She put her chin up, determined not to lose what little control she still possessed of the situation. "Whatever happened to the idea of playing by my rules?"

"Just let me know what they are," Keir agreed. "Last night, your rule book seemed to include such fascinating possibilities that I was happy to play along."

"Nothing happened last night." There was more bravado than certainty in her voice.

"Are you certain of that? Well, no matter. Are you changing the rules again? Have you decided you want Walter after all?"

"Of course not."

"Well, that's good. After last night, it would make things a bit difficult."

"Keir..." She didn't want to ask, but she couldn't stop. "What happened?"

"Ah," he said on a long note of satisfaction. "You really don't remember? You're quite a cuddler, you know—or maybe you don't. I suppose if you're not in the habit of sharing a bed, you might never have realized..."

"That's it." Jessica stood up. "It's obvious that nothing really happened last night, and I'm not listening to any more suggestive nonsense."

"Jess—"

She stopped at the door. "If this is the start of an apology, Keir, you waited just a little too long. Let me tell you right now—"

"Oh, I'm not apologizing," Keir said comfortably. "I just want to know if you sleep with a teddy bear when you're at home."

"Of course not!"

"Then I'll buy you one as soon as we're back in Kansas City."

Jessica tried to bite her tongue, but the question popped out anyway. "Why?"

He smiled. "Because I'd hate to have you be unhappy when you don't have me to hug any more."

It had been a couple of years since Jessica had played tennis—once Clementine got sick, there hadn't been time for her tennis club membership, and later there was neither money nor leisure.

So it was no surprise that her reactions were slow for a few games, or that she was breathing hard long before the first match point. At least, she told herself that the problem was her long absence from the sport and the fact that Lorna and Trevor, on the opposite side of the net from Walter and Jessica, were in top form.

It had nothing to do with Keir's sudden appearance on the terrace overlooking the court, where he lounged in a lawn chair and watched the action.

Still, when the second match was over and Walter announced with a laugh that it was time to quit because he couldn't keep up with the young people, Jessica wasn't quite sure whether she was relieved or apprehensive. At least on the court there hadn't been a chance for conversation.

She draped a towel around her neck and said to Trevor, ''That's a wicked backhand you've got. You must have developed it playing racquetball.''

Lorna was dabbing delicately at her face. ''Trevor doesn't play racquetball,'' she said flatly.

''My mistake.'' Jessica's voice was cool. She doubted that he would have lied to Lorna about something so unexceptional as racquetball. It wasn't as if the sport was dangerous. It wasn't even something Lorna would have perceived as lower class. Which indicated that his Tuesday racquetball dates had been entirely fictional.

Jessica wondered if that was when he'd been seeing Lorna, or if there was yet another hidden corner of Trevor's life. What would he say if she asked him about Tuesdays?

She dismissed the idea rather reluctantly. It wasn't that she cared so passionately about finding the truth, but it might have been interesting to watch Trevor squirm.

She dropped into a chair on the terrace and raised a bottle of spring water to her lips just as Keir said, ''It's too bad we can't offer you anything as exciting as tennis, Walter, or as nice as this weekend is. I'm afraid we'll have to settle for an ordinary dinner party. Perhaps you can come to our apartment one evening this week?''

Jessica choked. It was bad enough that she'd never seen Bernie's sister's apartment, but for all she knew, neither had Keir. And he was inviting people to dinner? Didn't he realize the kind of trouble he was asking for?

''Now that sounds lovely,'' Walter drawled. ''I suppose you're going to tell me that your little lady is a great cook.''

Keir said, without a flicker, ''Gourmet, of course.''

''Now that doesn't surprise me. My mother always said a good homemaker had to be able to do everything herself, so she could properly supervise the help. I imagine your family taught you the same sort of thing, Jessica?''

Jessica still hadn't caught her breath. All she could do was nod a halfhearted agreement.

''I'll be looking forward to it,'' Walter went on. He was practically rubbing his hands together in glee. ''Shall we say Tuesday?''

She tried to protest, but all that emerged was a croak.

Keir said, ''Of course. At seven? I'll give you the address. And we'd like Lorna and Trevor to come, of course.''

''How thoughtful of you,'' Lorna murmured. ''And perhaps the Jacksons, too.'' She raised her voice and called across the terrace, ''Oh, Maddy, here's your chance to see Jessica's home!'' She smiled at Jessica, but no warmth reached her eyes. ''Even if you don't exactly live in a mansion anymore, I'm sure Maddy will enjoy...'' She paused and added without a flicker, ''Oh, how thoughtless of me to invite extras. Do you have room at your table?''

For one instant, Jessica wondered almost hysterically what the reaction would be if she told the truth and admitted that she had never seen the apartment Keir was claiming was theirs. She wouldn't even bet that Bernie's sister owned a table, much less guess how many people she could seat around it.

She shot a look at Keir, hoping for some signal, but he was absorbed in conversation with Walter.

She mentally crossed her fingers and said, "Of course." Her voice was still just a little hoarse from her coughing attack. "Maddy, we'd be delighted to have you and your husband join us."

I'm nuts, she thought. What was she going to do if the place was hopeless?

The butler came to announce lunch, and as the others crossed the terrace Jessica hung back a little and gestured at Keir to join her.

He paused beside the French doors that led into the side hall, and Jessica noted, with annoyance, that he looked quite pleased with himself.

"That was neatly done, don't you think?" he said softly.

"About as neatly as a hangman's noose. Have you ever been in this apartment?"

"Now and then."

"Well, that's some relief."

"What's the matter, Jess?"

"Oh, nothing much," she said wryly. "It's just that before I plan a dinner party, I'd like to know if there's an actual dining room."

"Of course there is."

"Does it have a real table and chairs? I mean, Bernie's sister hasn't substituted couches like the ancient Romans used?"

''Not unless she's redone the place since the last time I was there,'' Keir said thoughtfully. ''I don't *think* she'd—''

''Well, since this is Bernie's sister, nothing would startle me. And considering how you surprised me with this—''

''But the dinner party was your idea, Jess.''

''Yes, it was. But I intended to wait till we'd at least looked at the apartment. That way we could always go back to Plan B and take them to Felicity's.''

''Carole's not like Bernie.''

''Now that's a surprise,'' Jessica muttered. ''I suppose you've invited Bernie to the dinner party, too?''

''Not yet. Would you like me to?''

''I think we have enough to handle as it is.''

''No doubt you're right. I suppose we'd better go in to lunch before we're missed. And by the way, if you'd like to hear about the chat about software that Walter and I had this morning over breakfast—''

Jessica wheeled to face him. ''You talked to him? And you didn't tell me?''

''I was going to,'' Keir said apologetically, ''but you seemed to prefer Walter and tennis to having a heart-to-heart with me, so—''

''What did he say?''

Keir glanced at his watch. ''Oh, he's interested. That's why I went ahead with the dinner invitation, because it's really just a matter of dangling the carrot a little closer to his nose. Speaking of which, have you made up your mind yet?''

Jessica's temper edged toward the breaking point. ''About whether I want to be the carrot?''

''I wouldn't have put it quite that crudely,'' Keir protested. ''I was just going to ask if you'd decided whether it was going to be him or me.''

"Neither," she snapped. "In fact, I can't wait for the day I see the last of both of you!"

The strain of the weekend had drained Jessica's reserves, and she slept a good part of the way back to Kansas City. When she stirred and sat up, they were already in the suburbs, and her neck was stiff. She rubbed it and groaned.

"That was quite a nap," Keir observed. "One would think something had kept you from resting properly all weekend."

"It was the book, no doubt." Jessica tried to sound careless.

"Since you enjoyed it so much, I'll get you a full set of the author's works, as well as the teddy bear."

"Oh, that's all right." Her voice was dry. "I wouldn't want to have my mind taken off business just now, and I'm afraid the books would be too tempting."

Keir didn't comment, but a tiny smile tugged at the corner of his mouth. "Do you want to stop at your place first and pick up the rest of your clothes?"

"No. What I'd like to do is see the apartment and then go home. To *my* home, by myself."

His eyebrows lifted. "What changed your mind, Jess?" He sounded quite concerned. "Something must have, because you didn't cuddle last night, and on the drive today you put your head against the car window rather than on my shoulder—that's why you woke up with a stiff neck, you know. What have I done to upset you?"

"I said that's what I'd like, not what I insist on doing."

"Oh, that makes me feel much better," Keir murmured. The car swept into a lavish apartment complex and drew up at the gate house. "Bernie was supposed to leave the key with the security guard—let's see if he remembered.''

The guard leaned out with a smile. "Good afternoon, Mr. Saunders. Mr. Morgan said you'd be along to get Miss Carole's key."

Keir dropped the key in his pocket and wheeled the Porsche down a twisting lane and around a number of corners to the building at the farthest corner of the development. He showed no hesitation about the complicated route, Jessica noted. He hadn't asked for directions at the gate. And there was no question in her mind that it was Keir the guard had recognized, not Bernie's Porsche.

As Keir parked the car in front of the building, she said, "And just how long did you date *Miss Carole,* Keir?"

Keir laughed. "Darling," he said gently, "you actually sound jealous. What a comfort it is to know that you care after all!"

Before any party, no matter how casual or elaborate, Jessica's stomach fluttered in nervousness. Would her guests enjoy themselves? Had she made the best choices for their entertainment? Had she overlooked something obvious that might be uncomfortable for them or embarrassing for her? After the dozens of parties in which she'd been involved, she'd gotten used to the reaction, though she would never find it comfortable.

On Tuesday evening, however, as she walked through the apartment for a final check before the Wyatts arrived, the flutters were more like aftershocks.

In the kitchen, coq au vin simmered gently. In the dining room, silver flatware gleamed against raw silk place mats on a huge glass-topped table. In the gate house, the security guard was waiting with directions for their guests.

Jessica had done everything she could think of to make the party go smoothly, but she knew these quivers would only go away when the guests did.

At least the apartment was ready. She still gave a sigh of relief each time she walked through the sun-drenched rooms or sank into one of the deep, overstuffed chairs. Carole Morgan's apartment was the kind of place Jessica would love to have for herself—stylish, but casual enough to be comfortable, with an indefinable air of youth and vigor. It was undisputedly feminine—in fact, it resembled a spring garden, with pastels of all shades juxtaposed almost at random—but the furnishings weren't at all frilly or fussy. Keir looked quite at home there.

Which, Jessica freely admitted, still bothered her a bit. Particularly because he seemed to know his way around the bedroom wing quite well, but he didn't have a clue where to find anything in the kitchen.

She wasn't jealous, of course. Keir was completely wrong about that. It was just that under different circumstances, she could have seen herself being friends with Carole Morgan, and she hoped that Keir, or Bernie, perhaps, had told Carole the truth.

Not that it mattered, of course, since Jessica would probably never meet the woman. Still...

She walked to the grand piano and picked up a silver-framed photograph of a young couple. Carole with her brother Bernie, Keir had told her on their first walk though the apartment on Sunday evening. There were a dozen similar photos of a dozen different young men. Keir wasn't among them, but instinct told her he probably had been once.

And if Jessica didn't want to answer questions about why she kept so many pictures of handsome young men around, she'd better move them before the doorbell rang.

She was carefully placing the frames in the hidden compartment of the piano bench when Keir called from down the hall, "Jess! If you're not busy, could you give me a hand for a second?"

The door of the master bedroom stood open, and just inside Keir was struggling with the starched French cuff of a formal shirt. "Help," he said. "I managed one cuff, but I can't get this one to fold right. And the studs won't go through the buttonholes, either."

Jessica concentrated on the cuff, trying to ignore the scent of his cologne and the texture of his skin as her fingertips brushed his wrist. The sparkling white of the formal shirt made his long, well-shaped hands look even more sensitive and sensual.

"I've never seen so much starch in one place outside of a pasta restaurant," Keir complained. "I can't believe guys wear these things any oftener than they have to."

"Most of them don't." She forced the cuff link through the hole and turned her attention to the studs that took the place of buttons on the shirtfront. It was an intimate sort of task, sliding each clip under the shirt, where the hair on his chest tickled her fingers, and fitting it through two matching buttonholes, starched so stiff they yielded only with force.

He was watching her, his head bent over hers so closely that his breath stirred her hair, and Jessica couldn't keep her fingers from trembling. She almost dropped one of the pearlescent studs, but eventually they were all in place.

She started to step away from him, but Keir's hands came to rest on her shoulders, holding her a foot from him while he looked her over from head to toe. His eyes were dark and intense.

"Nice dress," he said softly.

She skimmed a hand over her hip. The hunter-green silk felt as light as a breath, and the full-cut skirt swirled around her when she moved. "Are you certain Carole won't mind me wearing it?"

"Of course she won't mind. She told Bernie we could use whatever we needed."

"Her furniture's one thing, but her clothes... But of course I really don't have much choice. I can't wear the same dress every time I see the Wyatts, but it would blow our whole budget to buy something like this."

"Stop worrying about it, Jess. Carole's pretty easygoing."

The warmth in his voice annoyed her. "If she's so wonderful, why did you ever stop seeing her?"

Keir looked quizzical. "Who says I did?"

Jessica felt as if all the air had suddenly been sucked from the room. "Oh," she said. "Well...I just assumed—"

Keir smiled. It was a gentle smile, not a conceited one. He looked as if he understood—and that made Jessica even more annoyed with herself.

Almost imperceptibly, he was drawing her closer. His hands on her shoulders seemed to have melted the hunter-green silk and left him touching bare, sensitive skin.

She looked at him and swallowed hard, and admitted that she wouldn't mind at all if he kissed her. At least, she wouldn't mind if he was serious—not just toying with her because Carole wasn't available.

She found herself an inch closer. The starched front of his shirt was slick under her palms.

"Keir, why didn't you ask Carole to play this part?" Her voice was little more than a whisper.

He shrugged. ''She could hardly do it from Paris, could she?''

Jessica's self-esteem deflated just a little more. He'd thought it out, then. She wasn't just a make-believe wife, but a second-choice one as well.

The knowledge brought something very close to despair. Tears stung her eyes as she admitted that Keir had been right the night they'd moved into the apartment. She *was* jealous, but not only of Carole Morgan. She resented any other woman who might have held a place in his life, as well. And she dreaded the thought of the women who might be in his future long after he'd forgotten Jessica....

When, she asked herself miserably, had she fallen in love with him?

CHAPTER NINE

IN ANOTHER instant there would be no space left between them. Keir had inched Jessica closer, and he was looking at her lips. His gaze was as caressing as a touch, and Jessica wanted nothing more than to melt against his strength, to lose herself in the pleasure of his kiss. To pretend that she meant as much to him as he did to her...

But she knew that make-believe wouldn't be enough.

She didn't have the strength to pull away, but with the last spark of her self-control she turned her head, breaking the power of his mesmerizing gaze. Her eyes fell on Keir's favorite battered gray sweater, tossed in a heap on the blanket chest at the foot of the bed.

"You know," she said, trying to sound matter-of-fact, "it might be a good idea for me to bring some of my things in here from the guest room."

"Whatever you'd like," Keir murmured. His lips brushed a wisp of hair from her temple. "You can drape your satin jammies on my bedpost any time you want."

She closed her eyes in pain. How much she would like him to mean that. How easy it would be to let herself believe...

He said, against her ear, "Shall I help you move right now?"

"I only meant—" Jessica had to steady her voice and begin again. "It just occurred to me that this whole room looks pretty masculine at the moment. Since our guests will be using this bath, maybe some cosmetics scattered around would make it more convincing."

"How terribly disappointing," Keir murmured. He let her go and casually shrugged into the jacket of his tuxedo. "But I suppose you have a point, since they'll no doubt be ringing the bell at any moment."

And that, she reminded herself, was all his offer had meant to him—a teasing way to pass a few moments before the real business of the evening got under way.

"I talked to my mother again today," he added briskly as he straightened his cuffs. "She's determined to meet you."

Jessica sighed. The idea of meeting Keir's family was no less frightening than it had ever been, but suddenly there was an element of longing mixed with the dread. If things were slightly different, it could be her family, too...

Stop it right there, she told herself. There was no sense in letting herself dream of impossibilities. It was bad enough that she'd allowed herself to fall in love with Keir. To forget that there was nothing normal about this entire situation would only compound the pain she'd suffer when it ended.

"That's a really bad idea, Keir." She tried to keep her voice level, casual. "It'll only cause a lot of questions later."

"You're welcome to try to convince her of that."

"Can't you put it off for a while longer?"

Keir shook his head. "I'm afraid not. If we don't show up this weekend, she'll no doubt drop by Toolshop. So it's a question of whether you'd rather meet her unexpectedly or when you've had a chance to prepare yourself."

Jessica could see the sense in that. "What's so important about this weekend? If you could put it off for another week or two, maybe—"

"It's my parents' wedding anniversary."

"Oh. I remember you saying something about that, but I thought you were just making it up for Walter Wyatt's benefit. Well, I suppose if there isn't any choice..."

He smiled at her and flicked a careless finger against her cheek. "You're a rock, Jess."

The casual commendation affected her more sharply than anything else he'd ever told her—because this he clearly meant. She'd never dreamed she'd see the day, Jessica thought wryly, when being told she was solid and reliable would be far more important than a comment on how nicely she was dressed or how lovely her hair looked!

"It's only one evening, anyway," Keir added. "You can handle that with your hands tied behind your back."

Under ordinary circumstances, Jessica thought, he was right. But with the new and sudden realization that she loved him, how was she going to keep her balance? How could she spend an evening with the people who loved him most, pretending to be one of them—and yet not let herself forget that she must remain apart?

She'd think about that later, she decided—because in the meantime, she had a dinner party to get through, and she didn't dare let her mind wander.

Fred and Maddy Jackson were the first to arrive, and Keir was serving them cocktails when the Wyatts and Trevor came. Walter was in high good humor, and the moment his martini glass was in his hand he raised it to propose a toast. "Sorry, Fred," he said. "I hope it doesn't hurt your feelings too much, but your loss is my gain, and I plan to celebrate."

Jessica was puzzled. She shot a look at Keir, but he didn't seem to have any better idea than she did what was going on.

Fred Jackson laughed. "No, no. I'm glad to see Trevor starting to make a name for himself. He'll do a good job for you at Softek, and it's time he moved up from middle management and showed what he can do when he's in charge."

Jessica's heart froze. Trevor would be the new head of Softek? But that meant if Keir's plan succeeded, he'd be working for Trevor—and that would be just about the worst set of circumstances she could imagine.

As Walter began his formal toast, Jessica looked across the circle of guests to Keir. She sensed more than saw the momentary tightening of his mouth, and then he was smiling again and joining in the congratulations. She raised her wineglass with a hand that was only slightly · unsteady.

Keir hadn't known ahead of time. She'd swear he'd been as shocked by the news as she was. But Jessica was surprised at how quickly he'd recovered. Did he want the job—and the money—so very badly?

Of course he does, she told herself. He'd come so far; why would he draw the line at working for Trevor? Keir might not hold any great respect for the man, but he had no particular reason to resent Trevor, either. The fact that he'd as much as jilted Jessica wouldn't make an ounce's difference to Keir.

She excused herself to get a tray of appetizers from the kitchen. Alone for a moment, she leaned against the sink and tried to take deep breaths to calm herself. But her chest hurt too much. *Everything* hurt too much. Why couldn't she have held onto the peaceful denial of her feelings that had made the last week bearable?

Suddenly the idea of a single evening spent with his parents seemed a very minor event indeed. The real question was how she could make it through the weeks that remained until Keir's deal was either finalized or forfeited. How was she going to maintain the facade that let her pretend this was all still a game? And how, once they'd reached the end, was she going to face saying goodbye?

Over the coq au vin, Lorna turned the conversation to the Bennington family home. "Not that this isn't nice, of course, as apartments go," she said as she daintily speared an asparagus stalk and raised it to her lips. "But you must miss not only the house, Jessica, but everything that goes with it. Having to do everything yourself must be a dreadful nuisance. I know I simply couldn't function without Benson."

"Well, you'll have to, my girl," her father said. "Just because you're getting married doesn't mean I'm giving you my butler, too."

Lorna pouted prettily, but she didn't argue. However, Jessica wouldn't have bet anything against her eventual success.

"Heavens, it must be just like playing house for you," Maddy Jackson put in. "I remember, when Fred and I were first married, how much of an adventure everything was. Even washing the dishes together can be fun when you're in love."

Lorna looked a little doubtful about that. "But you're still planning to buy the Bennington house back, aren't you, Jessica?"

"Oh, I'm sure it's still in Keir's plans. But it will take some time to arrange the details," Jessica said, as easily as if she'd rehearsed the answer. "At least, he hasn't told me yet that it's not for sale—so I imagine he's hoping to surprise me."

The gleam in Keir's eyes as he met her gaze over the length of the table told Jessica that he fully appreciated how skillfully she'd danced around the truth, and for just an instant she was flooded with satisfaction.

Then once again her heart sank. How could she have failed to recognize that it wasn't simply a companionable bit of humor that made her feel so close to him in moments like these? She should have known long ago that what she felt for him was more than friendship, more than the shared danger of the scheme they'd embarked on.

"As Jess keeps telling me, everything is for sale at the right price," Keir said, and turned to Maddy Jackson.

"Well, you might not have as much competition from other buyers, since you're the last of the family," Lorna murmured.

"Just don't let them know you're sentimental about it," Walter advised, "or the price will go sky-high."

Fred Jackson put his fork down. "You don't have family, Jessica? Cousins, maybe?"

"No." The reply sounded curt, and Jessica tried to soften it. "At least, not that I'm aware of."

Fred chuckled. "And you're wondering why I should care, right? It's funny, though—the first time I met you, there was something about you that seemed familiar. But I couldn't put my finger on it—not till today."

Jessica kept smiling, but her face felt stiff. She'd thought this particular danger was past, since Fred had said nothing all weekend. What inconvenient twist of fate had reminded him now? And precisely what was it he remembered? Had he seen her with Trevor after all but convinced himself that it must have been a relative instead of Jessica?

As if he'd read her mind, Fred added, "It was your name that rang bells. Jessica Bennington reminded me of something, or someone, I couldn't place. It wasn't till today that I remembered."

Lorna was watching him with rapt attention. "Go on, Fred," she urged. "Tell us."

Jessica wondered if Lorna would be quite so fascinated if it turned out that Fred's memories included Trevor. She shot a look down the table at Keir. He appeared unconcerned—but then, she thought, he might not realize how damning the possibilities were.

"I thought perhaps you were related to someone my company's been looking for lately."

The remark came as such an anticlimax that Jessica couldn't even feel relief. "Sorry, Fred, but I don't think—"

"I didn't know Union Manufacturing was into missing persons now," Lorna said with something just short of a sneer.

"Only when they're stockholders who have dropped out of sight," Fred said crisply.

Walter snorted. "And you're worried about that? Every company has some of those. With this hostile takeover you're facing, I'd have thought you had better things to do than look for—" He paused and looked thoughtful.

"We do," Fred agreed. "Except in this case, the account was set up years ago, before Union Manufacturing was even organized, with just a few shares of stock in one of our predecessor companies. We lost track of the owner years ago, and apparently the owner lost track of the stock, too, or thought it had lost all its value in the buyout. At any rate, the account's been idle, except for the dividends being reinvested every quarter."

"And that reinvestment, along with the mergers and reorganizations the company's gone through..." Walter mused.

"It's grown into quite a nice chunk of Union Manufacturing, and in the midst of a takeover fight, we need every stockholder proxy we can get our hands on.'' Fred turned to Jessica. ''So when I heard your name, I thought perhaps you might know something about my missing person. She's also Jessica Bennington, you see, though she's got another name tacked on, as well.''

Keir cut a bite of coq au vin and raised it to his lips. His hands appeared perfectly steady, and his voice was level. ''It wouldn't be Marschall, by any chance? With a C in the middle?''

Fred's jaw dropped. He didn't have to answer. Jessica could see the confirmation in his eyes, and her wineglass tipped out of a suddenly nerveless hand. The delicate stem snapped, and cabernet splashed on the glass table, but Jessica didn't notice.

Keir's eyes met hers. ''Well, what do you know, Jess,'' he said gently. ''That what's-mine-is-yours bit in the wedding ceremony may have been an even better idea than I thought.''

It was just after midnight when the last of their guests left, and Jessica considered abandoning the mess to be dealt with the next morning. But her nerves were humming, and she knew she wouldn't sleep, so she pitched in.

Keir got a tray and helped to clear the dining room table.

''You don't have to do that,'' she told him. ''I enjoy cleaning up after a party. Getting everything clean and straight again helps relax me.''

''Do you suppose it'll work on me? I could use a little relaxation myself.'' He started haphazardly stacking dishes.

''Well, take it easy with the crystal, all right? I've already broken one glass, and that's enough.'' She ran the sink full of hot water and started to wash the brandy snifters.

When Keir carried the loaded tray into the kitchen, he was whistling, and the cheerful sound rubbed Jessica's nerves raw. "You're certainly happy," she commented. "Considering the problems with the Softek deal—"

"What problems? It's still a good deal for Walter, and he cornered me after dinner and said he's no less interested."

She was speechless.

"You look stunned, Jess. Did you think he was going to give the rising executive full control?"

"Why shouldn't he?" she snapped. "If Walter trusts Trevor enough to put him in charge in the first place—"

"Apparently he doesn't." He whistled another brief phrase and broke off. "Besides," he added blithely, "from what Fred said tonight, you've already hit the jackpot. Even if the Softek deal falls through, we won't have anything to worry about."

There was something about the casual way he linked the two of them that stung Jessica's pride, and her voice was sharp. "I don't think you should count your dividends just yet, Keir."

He dried a wineglass and set it aside. "And I don't think I like the sound of that," he said finally.

She shouldn't have been annoyed. She'd known all along that money, whatever its source, was an important factor to him. "I just meant that it's probably not anything enormous. I could be out of cash by the time I replace the glass I broke and have the wine stains cleaned out of Carole's dress."

"I doubt it, or Fred wouldn't have been looking for you. And even if your grandmother wouldn't have considered it a proper Bennington fortune, that doesn't mean it's anything to scoff at.''

There was an edge to his voice that she didn't understand. Of course she wasn't scoffing at the money. The truth was she was afraid to let herself count on anything substantial for fear she'd end up disappointed when she should be grateful for any amount at all.

''I'll bet the rising executive wouldn't turn it down,'' Keir went on.

Irritation at the implication that she still wanted Trevor burned up any desire she'd felt to explain herself. Jessica almost snapped at him that she was not, after all, an idiot, that the only way she'd have any interest in Trevor McIntyre right now was if his head was mounted on a silver platter.

She was already forming the words, in fact, when she realized that to say anything of the sort might make Keir question what had apparently changed her mind. And that might lead him to all kinds of uncomfortable insights.

Long ago, rather than further shred her dignity, she'd allowed him to think that Trevor was still important to her. Now she was paying the price.

She rinsed the last wineglass, set it up to drain and said crisply, ''That's a consideration, of course. I'll certainly have to think it over before I agree to cut you in for half.''

Fred Jackson explained the main points to Jessica the next morning in his office, and the more personal details weren't difficult to deduce.

Her father had set up the account when Jessica was no more than an infant. Her mother, she thought, might never have known of it. By Bennington standards in those days, the few dollars Bryan Marschall had scraped together for his daughter would have been almost laughable.

And since their later divorce had been both protracted and bitter, Jessica had no trouble imagining why he'd kept silent about what had been only a minor detail in their lives.

But it touched her that he'd never drawn a cent out of the account. Even in the years when he'd barely seen his daughter, he'd held onto the legacy he'd established for her.

Fred Jackson told her that the stockholder services division had mailed statements to Bryan Marschall at regular intervals. He'd moved around a lot, though, and it had not been unusual for him to respond only when his address changed. Only after an extended period with no contact at all, when an envelope finally came back marked Deceased, did the company realize they had no other address for the actual owner—Jessica herself.

That had been more than ten years ago. The amounts weren't large, and every publicly owned corporation had inactive accounts and careless stockholders who had lost track of their holdings. It was more of a nuisance than anything else.

So the account had remained dormant, and in the past decade it had quietly grown through mergers and buyouts and new products that had sent Union Manufacturing stock soaring—until the threat of a hostile takeover prompted an attempt to contact every person who owned as much as a single share.

Jessica's holdings were considerable, though the bottom line came nowhere close to the millions Keir had speculated they could clear on the Softek deal if everything went well. Still, it was a very nice chunk of cash— enough that Jessica could take all the time she wanted to choose a permanent career.

She was still in a daze when she left Fred Jackson's office, turning down his offer of lunch in the directors' dining room because she thought anything she tried to eat would choke her. She needed to be alone, not only to consider the impact the money would have on her life but to reassess the father she had always been told had practically abandoned her.

He had loved her, after all, this man she'd never had a chance to know—and that knowledge began to heal a crack she'd never realized lay hidden deep in her heart.

Her preoccupation was no doubt why she didn't see Trevor in the lobby until she almost bumped into him.

"Well, if it isn't the missing heiress," he said irritably. "Now, that's just my luck, isn't it? Finding out about you too late."

"It's not my fault you didn't do your research carefully enough, Trevor. Anyway, you surely don't mean you'd prefer me to Lorna now."

"Of course I would. You've got full control of your money. I did a little asking around the stockholders' services offices this morning, and—"

Jessica was hardly listening. "Believe me, Lorna has infinitely more cash than I do."

Trevor shook his head. "Not really. All she's got is what she can wheedle out of her daddy. The rest is only potential."

"Oh, I'm sure if you do a good job at Softek, Walter will make sure you're well compensated."

In one clipped sentence, Trevor gave her his unadulterated opinion of Softek.

If it hadn't been for Keir's involvement, Jessica would have been mildly amused, despite the profanity. She herself couldn't have dreamed up a better plan of revenge for Trevor than handing him full responsibility for a business he hated, then holding him accountable if he fell short of expectations.

In fact, she mused, the scheme was so perfect that she couldn't help wondering if Walter Wyatt might be thinking along precisely those lines. Walter was cunning enough not to openly oppose his daughter's choice, but he wouldn't stand by idly, either. If he suspected what Trevor had just told her, he might be giving the young man enough rope to hang himself in order to convince Lorna to give up her engagement.

At any rate, Jessica wouldn't have cared what happened, except for the effect the whole thing could have on Keir. Whether Walter knew what he was doing or not, Softek was likely to take a nosedive with an unwilling executive at the helm. And if Keir went into that situation without realizing the dangers Softek faced . . .

"I don't suppose you'd reconsider?" Trevor asked hopefully. "I could stay right here, vote your Union Manufacturing stock and eventually take over Fred's job."

Jessica was dumbfounded. Did the man's ego have no limits at all? She didn't even bother to answer, just walked past him and out of the lobby.

On the street, she automatically turned toward the nearest bus stop, then raised a hand and hailed a cab instead. With her first dividend check in her purse, she could well afford it.

Heedless of the cityscape speeding by, she sat in the cab and studied the emerald in Bernie's grandmother's ring. The stone shattered the sunlight into rays of blue and yellow and deep, intense green. Next to the emerald, subdued in comparison to its magnificence, the thin, plain gold wedding ring seemed to mock her.

What kind of a ring would Keir have given her if their engagement had been real? "A cigar band, probably," she muttered.

The cabbie said, "Ma'am?"

Jessica didn't realize she'd spoken aloud. "Nothing. It's that building there. The small one in the middle of the block."

Toolshop looked just the same. The outer office was deserted, but a small stack of unopened mail waited on her desk. Jessica flipped through the envelopes and decided to let them wait till she could concentrate. The scent of overbrewed coffee hung in the air. She dumped the black, tarry liquid from the pot and made a fresh batch. When it had finished brewing, she poured a cup and took it into Keir's office.

His attention was focused on the computer screen, and for almost a minute Jessica stood inside the door, studying the back of his head till she thought she could draw the pattern of his curls.

How could she have stood there, day after day in the not-so-distant past, and not realized how she felt about him?

She had to take a deep breath before she could even try to speak, and a wave of longing swept over her for the time just a few weeks ago when she'd been able to be herself with him. Now she had to guard every word, every intonation, for fear he would hear in her voice the truth she needed so badly to hide from him and from the world.

It was bad enough to love him. To let him know that for her the scam had become all too real would be the final crushing blow to her pride.

Keir rubbed a hand across the back of his neck as if it hurt, and Jessica's fingertips tingled with the desire to massage those tense muscles. There was nothing sexual about the urge to touch him—

And she was lying to herself about that, too, she admitted. She could feel desire rising at the mere thought of walking across the room and laying her palms against his skin. What would have happened if during that weekend at the lake she had turned to him instead of picking up a book? Would she now have regrets—or memories to cherish?

Don't think about it, she told herself. The opportunity was gone, and she would only cause herself more pain by wondering what it would have been like to make love with him.

She set his coffee beside the keyboard.

He looked up. "Hi. I wasn't expecting you back so soon."

Was that a somber question in his eyes? "It didn't take long," she said. "Just some papers to sign."

"Was it worth the trip?" He sounded almost casual, but Jessica could hear something very like strain under the words.

"You could say that." She tried to smile. "Grandmother might have considered it worthy of a Bennington after all."

His shoulders slumped. Some of the tension seemed to have drained out of him, Jessica thought. She could take care of the rest in an instant simply by telling him that she'd stick to the original agreement—half of everything she possessed would be his.

But he was already focusing on the computer again. "That's great, Jess." He pulled the keyboard closer.

"Don't you want to hear the details?"

"Maybe later. Right now I've got another hour's work to do."

She glanced at the screen, but it didn't tell her anything. "The new program?"

"No, it's the realtor's package. When I talked to him this morning, I promised to get it to him before the end of the day."

"Then I'll let you finish, and we'll discuss this later."

"Thanks for the coffee, Jess."

She was at the door when he spoke again, without looking up. "You looked a little nervous when you came in."

She tensed. "Did I?"

Keir nodded. "Did you come in to tell me you're quitting?"

Leave him? The idea struck her heart like the slash of a knife. "Why would I quit?" she said levelly. "We have a job to finish, remember? The agreement was that until the Softek deal is completed or dead—"

"You did say a couple of weeks ago that you were looking for something else to do."

That was before I knew how much you mattered. The words echoed in her head so clearly that for an instant Jessica was afraid she'd said them aloud. "I'll stick around," she said finally, and added, to salve her pride, "for a while, at least."

She was working her way through the mail—mostly bills, with a few orders sprinkled in—when Keir came out of his office a little later, a pack of computer disks in his hand. "It shouldn't take long to get this up and running." He tossed the disks from one hand to the other and added casually, "How about dinner at Felicity's tonight?"

A long, romantic dinner, Jessica thought, at the first place they had ever gone together... She hesitated. Could she bear it if the evening didn't mean as much to him as it would to her?

Keir seemed to feel her misgivings. "You can tell me all about Fred then."

"Not Felicity's," she said, as if the words had been forced from her.

His eyes narrowed. "You name the place, then. I'll be back soon."

The door banged behind him, and Jessica put her head in her hands. Under this kind of pressure, how long could she keep on? And yet, the thought of giving up even a moment with him—no matter how painful—was even worse.

By forcing herself to concentrate on the work that had been put off while she prepared for their dinner party, she got through the next couple of hours. She was surprised when the front door opened. She hadn't thought Keir would be back so soon.

But it wasn't him. Instead, Walter Wyatt stood just inside the office, looking around with undisguised interest and a whisper of contempt.

"Hello, Walter," she said. "I'm afraid Keir's out of the office this afternoon. If you'd like to wait—"

"I really came to talk to you, Jessica."

She had already come around her desk to offer him a cup of coffee, and she looked at him curiously. There was something about his tone...

His gesture encompassed the entire small room. "Have you really convinced yourself you can be happy with this?" he asked almost wistfully.

Jessica's hand shook, slopping the hot liquid over the edge of the mug. "Walter, I don't—"

"The man's got some talent, yes—and with your strength and determination behind him, he might make something of himself someday. But—"

"Walter, please don't insult Keir."

"I'm not insulting him. I'm asking an honest question, Jessica. Is this the way you want to live?" He took the mug, set it aside and pulled a white handkerchief from his pocket to wipe the hot drops of coffee from her fingers. "How I wish I'd met you earlier," he said softly. "You're everything I've looked for all these years."

Jessica's hands were trembling.

"I know you don't love me, and that's all right. But if you're determined to marry for advantage, Jessica, at least choose someone who can give you something worthwhile."

A level voice spoke from the doorway. "Like you, Walter?" Keir crossed the room and picked up the discarded coffee.

Walter eyed the mug warily. "Like me," he said firmly. "Come now, Keir, let's be reasonable. It's not too late to straighten out this mess."

"What do you suggest? A quick game of poker, winner take all? Or will simple coin flipping do?"

Jessica found her voice. "Don't be absurd, Keir. I'm not anyone's property. You said yourself that the rules were up to me, and I don't need your protection."

"You mean you want to listen to this garbage?"

He had her there, and Jessica couldn't deny it. But she couldn't back down, either. "It's absolutely absurd for you to butt in, Keir. I can take care of myself. Unless, of course, it's not me you're worried about so much as half of that nice little stock portfolio!"

The sapphire of his eyes suddenly went steel gray, and his voice was no less hard. "You know, Jessica, I don't like what having some money has done to you."

She wanted to say, *It isn't the money that matters, Keir.* She wanted to tell him that the stock was unimportant—except for what it could mean to him.

Everything's for sale at a price. Glib though the philosophy was, there was an undercurrent of truth to it. Perhaps even Keir was for sale.

She toyed with the idea of telling him right now that he could have every penny's worth of stock—if she could have him in return. He might agree to the deal. It would buy him a good portion of the financial freedom he wanted.

But though she might be able to buy him, Jessica knew she couldn't afford the price, for the purchase would cost her far more than money. It would cost her hope, and pride, and self-respect, and ultimately any chance for happiness. Unless he loved her as she loved him, there was no future worth looking toward. Money didn't begin to enter that equation.

What a great joke this had turned out to be. They had gone after a fortune—and now that she'd won it, the money wasn't worth anything at all.

It would hurt to walk away from him, but she knew in the long run to do anything else would hurt even worse—for if she tried to use the money to keep him beside her, she would ultimately lose not only him but herself.

CHAPTER TEN

BUT of course, Jessica couldn't tell him any of that. Keir had handed her a ready-made excuse—and though she shuddered at the idea of letting him believe her so selfish, it was better than allowing him to guess the truth.

So she said coolly, "I suppose it's in the blood. Once a Bennington, always a Bennington."

Keir's eyes narrowed. The sharpness of his gaze sent icicles sliding down her spine. Unable to look at him, she turned her attention to Walter. He was staring, his mouth hanging open, but suddenly he seemed to collect himself. "Well, I'd better run along," he said uncertainly, and edged toward the door. "Sorry if I caused problems."

"You didn't," Jessica murmured.

"Nothing to signify," Keir said at the same moment.

The door banged behind Walter, and the silence in the shop was complete. Keir didn't take his eyes off Jessica. She could feel the weight of his gaze.

It could only have been seconds, but it seemed like forever before she regained enough poise to say, "Don't you think you'd better go after him and explain?"

"Explain what? That I still want to deal? What's the matter, Jess? Are you afraid my macho pride might get in the way and make me pass up the opportunity after all?"

"And cheat me out of my half of those millions you promised," she agreed. Her voice was brittle. "You'd better hurry, or it'll be too late."

"Whatever you say." Keir turned at the door. "Just don't go anywhere. I have a few things to tell Walter, but that doesn't mean we aren't going to have a talk as soon as I get back. We're long overdue."

Cold fear gripped Jessica's heart. With almost automatic defiance, she said, "I'll go anywhere I like." But Keir was already out the door, and she didn't think he'd heard.

She wondered how long she had before he returned and what he planned to say. Her hands were shaking at the prospect, for she knew she couldn't indefinitely keep up the frail mask that was her only defense. If he turned his immense power of concentration on her...

The only thing she could do was run. With trembling fingers and one eye on the door, she composed a two-sentence letter of resignation. She left it propped on the computer keyboard in Keir's office, weighed down by Bernie's grandmother's emerald ring, and got her coat from the tiny closet.

Walter Wyatt's Cadillac was still parked beside the building when she slipped out the door and started down the street, but it was empty. Through the big plate-glass window of the deli, she caught a glimpse of him and Keir, seemingly absorbed in conversation. She thought neither of them saw her.

The deli was where this had all started, really, she reflected. Keir had soothed away her tears the morning after Trevor had made his grand announcement. He'd taken her out for breakfast and treated her gently—even warmly—when he thought she was suffering from morning sickness....

She smiled sadly, remembering how utterly furious she'd been with him over the mere suggestion. Now, the memory of his kindness brought a wave of longing for what might have been. If this had been a real marriage, she might be looking forward to a child someday.

Keir's child—who would no doubt be as uncomfortably precise as his father about the things that were important to him and as cheerfully oblivious of the ones that weren't. Just the prospect of answering such a child's questions about why the grass was green and the sky blue was a terrifying thought...and an exciting one. It was the kind of full-time job she could savor.

But it was nothing more than self-torture to think of a child who would never exist—a child who had never been a possibility at all. There was nothing to be gained by making herself even more miserable. It was time to pick up her life again.

She'd done it before, after Clementine's death. She'd done it after Trevor's betrayal. She could do it once more.

At least, that was what Jessica told herself, and maybe, with time, she might be convinced it was true. Maybe someday Keir Saunders would fade into nothing more than a memory.

If, she thought, she lived to be a hundred.

Perversely, now that Jessica could move almost anywhere she wanted, the studio apartment felt more like home than it ever had before. Besides, she told herself, there was no hurry about looking for another apartment. The silence would be the same no matter where she went.

She might not want to stay in Kansas City at all. There was nothing much to keep her in the Midwest, and a great deal of attraction in the idea of a fresh start somewhere else, in a place where Bennington was only a name. But she made no move toward deciding where she might want to live.

She knew, though she didn't want to admit it, that there was another, far more important reason for staying in the tiny apartment. If she moved, Keir wouldn't know where to start looking for her.

Not that he'd want to, she told herself. She was only fooling herself to think he might. If he'd really been set on having that talk, he'd have chased her down as soon as he'd found her letter. But since he hadn't...

She didn't want to talk to him anyway. She'd made that perfectly clear in the note she'd left. Of course, she wasn't fool enough to think that alone would have stopped him. Something had obviously changed his mind. Perhaps he was too busy working out a deal with Walter Wyatt to worry about petty details like Jessica and a marriage he no longer needed.

As the hours wore on and the weekend crept nearer, she found herself wondering how his negotiations were proceeding. Guiltily, she remembered that she ought to have told Keir what Trevor had said about Softek, and about her suspicion that the business would soon be on a fast downhill slide. She'd intended to, of course, but that final confrontation had driven the whole thing out of her mind.

Of course, if he and Walter had already struck a deal, it was too late for the warning. Keir might not even take her seriously.

Still, the knowledge weighed so heavily on her that by Friday afternoon, she could stand it no longer. Whatever the cost, she owed it to Keir to caution him. Even if he'd already agreed to some sort of bargain, at least he could protect himself from the worst of the fallout. And if he didn't listen...well, then she could tell herself that at any rate she'd tried.

Her wardrobe still held nothing to take the place of the pine-green suit she'd worn for her wedding. She hadn't had the urge to shop, since there didn't seem to be an occasion for new clothes.

And there wasn't any reason to dress up just to go talk to Keir, either, she told herself. But she needed all the confidence she could muster, so she put on the suit anyway.

She was still getting used to her little car, the only real indulgence she'd allowed herself in the few short days since she'd received her first check. It felt strange to have the freedom to follow her impulses, to go where she liked without considering transit routes and schedules.

One of those whims struck just as she passed the Bennington mansion on Ward Parkway, and before she really realized what she was doing, Jessica had turned onto the side street and pulled between the gates and into the drive.

A lawn service truck was parked near the garage, and she could hear the roar of a leaf blower from somewhere behind the house. A uniformed worker was wrapping Clementine's rosebushes to protect them from the winter's cold, and as Jessica watched, the front door opened and a woman came out to talk to him. She was very much the kind of woman Jessica would have expected— tall, painfully thin, expensively tailored, assured of her place in the world and not concerned what anyone else thought of her.

Jessica almost backed out. But she told herself it couldn't do any harm to ask, so she slid out of the car and crossed the lawn.

The woman turned. Her gaze flicked across the car and then assessed Jessica. "If you're looking for directions," she said curtly, "I doubt very much I can help. And if you're looking for work, I'd suggest an agency."

She's the kind of woman I might have turned into, Jessica thought, *if fate hadn't intervened.* She bit her tongue to keep from saying something equally rude, and said, "I was just wondering if the house might be for sale."

The woman's expensively plucked eyebrows soared. "As a matter of fact, it's not."

"Thank you," Jessica murmured.

Of course it wouldn't be. She knew from her own experience that people didn't lightly buy and sell houses like this one. In any case, even if the mansion was for sale, Jessica couldn't justify a purchase like that. It would consume too high a portion of her assets. Besides, it was a house for a family, not a single woman—and since, at the moment, despite the wedding ring she still wore, she couldn't imagine being anything but single...

In fact, she admitted, she'd probably only stopped because she was dawdling—putting off the difficult moment to come, when she would see Keir again.

Toolshop seemed to look even more tired than it had two days before. Of course, Jessica told herself, that was probably just a reflection of her own mood. The building couldn't possibly have started to sag in the mere forty-eight hours she'd been gone.

She parked the car in front, hesitated, lost her nerve and crossed the street to the deli instead, trying to ignore the voice in the back of her head that said her main objective at the moment wasn't a peace offering but a delay.

The clerk looked up from a newspaper and stepped to the counter. "Haven't seen you for a few days. Have you been on vacation?"

"Something like that. I'd like a peanut-butter-with-jelly-and-banana sandwich to go."

The clerk's jaw dropped, but she reached for the bread. "Not you, too?" she asked as she opened a jar of peanut butter. "Or are you shopping for the boss?"

"Has he been eating them regularly?" Jessica tried to keep her voice casual, but she remembered what the clerk had said long ago about Keir's tastes when he was working under pressure.

"Practically every night. There's been a lot of activity over there the last few days." The clerk wrapped the sandwich in waxed paper, dropped it in a bag and pushed it across the counter.

A lot of activity. That certainly indicated the deal was proceeding. Maybe there wasn't any point in going to talk to Keir. But she'd come this far—and besides, Jessica asked herself wryly, what on earth would she do with a peanut-butter-with-jelly-and-banana sandwich if she didn't give it to him?

The old computer had been moved onto the makeshift desk that had been Jessica's, and Randy was leaning back in her chair with his feet propped up, mouthing something. Jessica decided it must be the words to a song playing on his earphones.

When he saw her he jerked upright and pulled the earphones off. "Hey, Jess! You're back!"

"You have a talent for spotting the obvious, Randy. Where'd you get the new addition?" She pointed at a sign propped on the front of her desk. Shipping Department, it said in large, crude letters.

"Oh, we've actually been getting some orders."

"That's good. Is Keir in?"

Randy nodded. "Look, I'm sorry about tying up your desk, but I'm sort of busy at the moment." He leaned forward to pop a disk out of the computer, and with a smooth motion he inserted another one. A few efficient keystrokes started the drive working, and he settled into his chair once more.

The door of the inner office opened. "Randy, my new computer should be—'' Keir saw her and stopped on the threshold.

He was better dressed than she'd seen him before—at least in the office. The battered old sweater was nowhere to be seen, and he was almost as good-looking in dark gray flannel trousers and a navy sports coat as he'd been in his tuxedo.

The deal's been struck, she thought. *He's even adopted corporate dress.*

"Well," he said. "Did you come by to check on your share?"

Almost automatically, Jessica shook her head. Apprehension made her stomach feel like a vacant pit. Keir was obviously in no mood to be understanding about anything. He certainly wasn't likely to be magnanimous about why she was coming to warn him now instead of when the admonition could have done some good.

"I was just wondering about the legal paperwork," she said.

Keir stepped aside and pointed into his office.

Jessica clutched her paper bag as if it was a shield and went in. "Do you want to start the divorce, or should I?"

He closed the door and leaned against it.

"Keir?" she said finally. "We can't stay married forever."

"I suppose you're right. Go ahead, start it. Anything else?"

Jessica braced herself. This was what she had come for, after all. "I thought I should tell you—warn you, actually—that Trevor's not too happy with his new job." She opened the bag and laid the sandwich beside the keyboard.

Keir ignored it. "And he's been baring his soul to you?" He didn't wait for an answer. "Is there any particular reason I should care what the rising executive thinks?"

"Well, if you're going to work for him..."

"I'm not." His voice was almost harsh.

"The agreement fell through? But—"

Keir nodded.

"I suppose when Walter saw that fight we had... I'm so sorry."

"Are you? Well, I suppose you could have used the money. A little extra always comes in handy."

"Dammit, Keir, I don't care about the money!" She was almost shouting. "I know how much you wanted that deal—the time to work on your program, the freedom from financial worries..."

She felt rather than saw the way his body tightened, as if the stress was more than he could bear.

She took a deep breath. "Look, it's not anything like what Softek could have given you, but maybe I've got enough to help. If I sell my Union Manufacturing stock—"

"Your father invested that money for your future."

"So I'll invest it with you, instead."

He didn't look at her. "Why? Because you feel responsible?"

She hesitated, and then told the truth. "No. Because I want you to have your chance."

"And if I lose your money?"

She shrugged. "Then I won't be any worse off than I was before, will I?"

"No strings?"

She said, very quietly, "No strings." She wouldn't try to buy him. But if in the meantime he learned to care for her... that would be a different matter altogether.

"Jess," he said.

How much she'd missed hearing him call her that—but this time there was a softness in his voice that she'd never heard before, a softness that made her want to cry.

Don't mistake it for something more than gratitude, she warned herself. She had just handed him the opportunity he'd been working for. It would be so easy to mess up by hoping for more.

"That's all, then," she said. "I'll see about converting the stock into cash. It might take a while, but within a week or two, I think you can begin—"

"Jess," he said. "It's very sweet of you. But I don't want your money."

For a moment, she thought she couldn't have heard him correctly. *He has to take it,* she thought. Because if he didn't, there was no hope, nothing to keep the two of them connected.

And obviously that was the way Keir wanted it. There was nothing left to say. Jessica knew she should just walk away and save her dignity.

But she couldn't. "Half of it is yours anyway. That was the deal." She tried to put a smile in her voice. "What's mine is yours—remember?"

He smiled a little. "I'll settle for you going to dinner with me tonight."

"Dinner?" The suggestion was so unexpected that she almost laughed. "Why?"

"It's still my parents' anniversary."

"Oh, no. If you're planning for us to fight the whole time so everybody in your family will understand when we break up—" She could hardly form the words, she was so tired of playing a part. "I don't want to, Keir."

His voice was soft. "What do you want, Jess?"

She couldn't look at him. Absently, she picked up half of his peanut-butter-with-jelly-and-banana sandwich and took a bite. The combination was sticky. It made her tongue feel thick, but at least it gave her an excuse not to answer.

"Shall I tell you what I want?" Keir said. He had moved just a little closer.

The door swung open and banged against the desk. A dark-haired man carrying an enormous box shouldered his way past Randy and said cheerfully, "Hi, Keir. I knew you'd be anxious to play with the new computer, so I brought yours over before I even unpacked mine."

Jessica recognized him from the photograph in Carole Morgan's apartment. This, at long last, was Bernie.

He went on blithely, "That's not what you're wearing to the anniversary dinner, is it? Mother's going to be fried if you turn up looking like that. It's so formal she's even hired Jonathan back from Felicity's for the occasion—"

Jessica put down the sandwich and stood up, and for the first time Bernie saw her.

"Oh—hi," he said uncertainly. "You must be Jessica."

"And you're Bernie," she said coolly. "Carole Morgan's brother, Bernie. And—correct me if I'm wrong—Keir's brother, as well?"

"Only half," Bernie said hastily. "We have different fathers. I wouldn't want to claim any more of a relationship than I have to—I'm sure you understand that, being around Keir as much as you have."

"Of course I understand."

"Bernie," Keir ordered. "Get out."

"But I just— Okay. Where do you want me to put the computer?"

"Dump it in the Missouri River, all right? Just *get out*!"

Bernie left, the computer still in his arms.

Keir shut the door behind him. "Jess—"

She faced him squarely. "When were you going to tell me, Keir?"

"A couple of days ago—when I asked you to dinner at Felicity's."

The night she hadn't wanted to go, she remembered. The night she hadn't been able to face the memories of Felicity's and so had suggested they go somewhere else. The night that had never been, because Walter Wyatt had shown up, and they'd had a fight instead....

"Speaking of Felicity's," she said coolly, "what did Bernie mean, your mother hired Jonathan *back* for the occasion? No, don't bother to answer. No wonder he looked so pained at having to teach you the wine-tasting ritual. He knew perfectly well you didn't need to be taught!"

"I...Jess—"

"You didn't need me to guide you through society's rules."

"No."

"You know all of them already. It was all lies, wasn't it? Or would you rather just call it a good joke?"

"I won't deny I had some fun, but that wasn't why I did it."

"So why did you do it, Keir? Because you felt sorry for me—the poor little ex-rich girl? Because you thought it was a way to give me money?"

"Jess, no."

"I'm a great charity case, aren't I? Well, thanks for the effort, but I don't need your help anymore. I don't need *you* anymore!" And that was the biggest lie she'd ever told. Tears stung her eyes, and she reached blindly for a tissue. "*Why*, Keir?"

"Because I couldn't bear to let you go out of my life," he said steadily.

"Because I'm the best darned office manager you've ever had?" Jessica said bitterly.

"No." His voice was little more than a whisper. "Because you're the only woman I've ever loved."

She staggered as if the floor had suddenly moved under her feet.

"But you'd never even looked at me that way, had you, Jess?"

"I..." She stopped. He was right—and what could she say? That she'd been an idiot not to see months ago what he meant to her?

"The day I hired you," Keir went on, "the rising executive picked you up after the interview, and I watched the hug of celebration you gave him before you got into the car. It was always Trevor. And even when he jilted you—"

"I didn't still want him," she said defensively. "I'm not such a fool as that."

"Maybe not, but that doesn't mean you wanted me, either. If I'd told you the day you confided in me about him that I was in love with you—"

"I'd have dumped my coffee over your head and walked out," Jessica admitted. "I'd had it with men right about then."

"Give me credit for a little intuition," Keir said dryly. "But when you started talking about leaving Toolshop and looking for a better job... I had to stop you. If Walter Wyatt's three suits hadn't happened by, I'd have come up with something else."

She thought about that for a moment and said unsteadily, "I don't even want to contemplate the possibilities."

He smiled a little. "I'd considered some very innovative strategies—I'll tell you about them sometime. But I kept coming back to the idea of an engagement, or even a wedding, if I could pull it off. At least then you couldn't do something crazy on the rebound."

"Right. As if marrying you wasn't crazy enough." She sighed. "Keir, I'd have sworn the only thing you were interested in was striking that deal and making your millions. Then, when my financial situation changed just as your negotiations seemed to be falling apart—"

"Fred Jackson's bombshell hit me hard, Jess. Suddenly you didn't need me any more—and the money seemed so terribly important to you."

She swallowed hard. "There were so many people who only cared about me because of my name and the Bennington money. I couldn't bear to think you might be like them."

"Never," he said. "But I was torn. I didn't think I could have been so mistaken about you, and yet you kept pushing me away, practically telling me that the money was all that mattered—"

"I was afraid," she admitted. "Afraid that I'd try to buy you, even though I knew that if you didn't care about me, only the money, we'd both end up miserable."

"All the fuss about money," he said. "And neither one of us gave a damn about it after all."

She was in his arms by then, not quite sure how she'd gotten there but content just to be close to him, knowing that she could always lean against his strength. And when he raised her face to his and kissed her, softly and slowly, the desire that had for so long been simmering deep inside her began to boil, leaving them both breathless.

"I love you," she whispered.

Finally, with obvious reluctance, he lifted his head, but he pulled her even closer, pillowing his cheek against her hair. "My mother will really not understand if we don't show up at all," he said. "Since she knows that I've reached an agreement on the Softek deal, and I can't use business as an excuse any more—"

"An agreement? I thought you said the whole thing was dead."

"Oh, the megamerger is as cold as a corpse. What I agreed to is what Walter wanted from the beginning. He gets the rights to the program he was after—the one that's already on the Internet—and I'm keeping the new one to develop myself. I put out some feelers last week to check the interest level, and Randy's been busy ever since, so I think we're on a roll."

"He told me there were orders, but I thought—"

"There have been a couple of bags of mail already, and more e-mail traffic than he can handle. It's going to take off like wildfire, and we'll end up beating Softek at their own game, using Walter's money to fund the whole project. Isn't that a kick?" He grinned, and then sobered suddenly as he looked at her. "He deserves it for trying to take you away from me."

"You didn't seem to care."

"I cared. As long as you didn't take him seriously, I could laugh about it. But the minute you told me to mind my own business..." He ran his hands over her hair, and cupped his palms at the back of her head. "I need you, Jess."

"I suppose that means you want your office manager back?"

"That, too. But there's a far more important job for you—if you'd like it. I want a wife."

Her throat was too tight to speak, so she nodded.

"I'm sorry about your white wedding, darling. If you want, we can still work it out, you know."

"It's not the wedding that matters, Keir—it's the marriage."

He smiled slowly, and she felt her heart stretch to encompass all the love she felt for him.

Keir pulled the emerald ring out of his breast pocket. "Want this back?"

She looked at him doubtfully. "Are you certain Bernie won't mind?"

"He got the ruby, and Carole has the sapphires. Mother's still wearing the diamonds." Keir had the grace to look a bit ashamed of himself. "You know, I never really said the ring was Bernie's, Jess, just that it came from his grandmother."

"And since she was your grandmother, too..."

He nodded. "I couldn't come straight out and tell you the emerald was mine. You'd have had too many questions. But I wanted you to wear my ring. There was a secret tingling pride every time I looked at you—my wife." He kissed her long and slowly. "You know," he said thoughtfully, "you taste like peanut butter."

"Have a bite yourself, and you won't notice." Her voice was husky. "No wonder you said you hadn't stopped seeing Carole."

"My favorite—and only—sister." He pulled Jessica onto the couch, into the safe circle of his arms. "I was going to come over to your apartment this afternoon, by the way. I figured you'd had two days to cool off, so maybe you'd be willing to listen. And you hadn't returned your wedding ring, so I hoped..." He kissed her temple lightly. "I was going to confess everything and ask you to come to the anniversary party, to meet some people who are very important to me. Just in case you decided sooner or later that you might want to be part of the family, after all."

"I think I can manage to stay on my good behavior."

"I should hope so," he teased. "It's only one evening, and you *are* a Bennington. By the way, do you still want the house?"

Jessica was hardly listening. The softness of his breath as he nibbled at her earlobe was creating little ripples of sensation that made it very hard to concentrate.

"It wouldn't do me any good to want it," she said absently. "It's not for sale."

He pulled back for a moment to look at her. "You're right. But just how do you know that?"

"Because I stopped there today and asked the owner. I don't quite know why I bothered—"

"I think I do. Because it would make such a beautiful home for us."

"Yes." There was a whisper of sadness in her voice. "But so will a lot of other places. And maybe someday…" She slid an arm around his neck and tugged his head down till his lips met hers once more.

A long time later, he asked, "How were the lawn care people doing?"

"They were wrapping Grandmother's rosebushes." She paused. "Keir."

"Yes, my love?"

"How'd you know about the lawn care people?"

"Because you weren't talking to the owner. You were talking to the previous owner, who won't move out till next week."

"You—" She folded up a fist and shook it under his nose.

Keir laughed and kissed each knuckle.

"Where'd you get the money to buy the house? Getting a bagful of orders for your new program is wonderful news, but—"

"Oh, we haven't talked about that, have we? There's

a little matter of a trust fund. My grandfather, you see—''

''The same one who gave your grandmother the emerald ring?''

''And Bernie's ruby, and Carole's sapphires, and Mother's diamonds. He owned a string of jewelry stores.''

''Well, that was handy.''

''Also lucrative,'' he agreed. ''They still are, as a matter of fact. Socially we're nowhere near Bennington level, but financially—''

''No wonder you were never concerned about money. If you've always had it—''

''I never really gave it much thought, and I didn't realize till you started talking about quitting your job how worried you were. It was part of the fun to see if Toolshop could really support itself, and the fancy trappings that money can provide were never all that important to me. Now, of course—''

''You didn't have to buy the house for my sake,'' she said. ''Though I absolutely won't move into this office with you. If you want, though, we could make do in my apartment for a while.''

''That would be cozy—but I think we'll have to keep the house. You see, I've already given up the lease on this place, now that I have the garage I've always wanted.'' He kissed her once more, very slowly, and by the time he'd finished Jessica's nerves were throbbing. ''Jess, are you absolutely positive we can't stay married forever?''

She considered. ''Well, I'm willing to give it a try if you are.''

''Good,'' he whispered. ''Let's start real soon now.''

Jessica smiled and put her head on his shoulder.

MILLS & BOON®

Next Month's Romances

$\heartsuit$

Each month you can choose from a wide variety of romance novels from Mills & Boon. Below are the new titles to look out for next month from the Presents and Enchanted series.

Presents™

MISTAKEN FOR A MISTRESS	Jacqueline Baird
NIGHT OF SHAME	Miranda Lee
THE GUILTY WIFE	Sally Wentworth
LOOKING AFTER DAD	Elizabeth Oldfield
LOVERS' LIES	Daphne Clair
CLOSE RELATIONS	Lynsey Stevens
THE SEDUCTION TRAP	Sara Wood
HER PERSONAL BODYGUARD	Susan Mc Carthy

Enchanted™

THE DAUGHTER OF THE MANOR	Betty Neels
A BUSINESS ENGAGEMENT	Jessica Steele
RUNAWAY HONEYMOON	Ruth Jean Dale
McALLISTER'S BABY	Trisha David
BRIDE ON THE RANCH	Barbara McMahon
AMBER AND THE SHEIKH	Stephanie Howard
ONCE A COWBOY...	Day Leclaire
PRINCE OF DELIGHTS	Renee Roszel

RACHEL LEE

◇

A FATEFUL CHOICE

**She arranged her own death—
then changed her mind**

*"Ms Lee's talents as a writer are
dazzling. Put this author's name on
your list of favourites right now!"*
—Romantic Times

**AVAILABLE IN PAPERBACK
FROM MARCH 1997**

SANDRA BROWN

New York Times bestselling author

HONOUR BOUND

Theirs was an impossible love

"One of fiction's brightest stars!"
—Dallas Morning News

Lucas Greywolf was Aislinn's forbidden fantasy—and every moment of their mad dash across Arizona drew her closer to this unyielding man.

AVAILABLE IN PAPERBACK
FROM MARCH 1997

FREE!

FOUR FREE
specially selected
Enchanted™ novels
<u>PLUS</u> a FREE Mystery Gift
when you return this page...

Return this coupon and we'll send you 4 Mills & Boon® Enchanted™ novels and a mystery gift absolutely FREE! We'll even pay the postage and packing for you.

We're making you this offer to introduce you to the benefits of the Reader Service™– FREE home delivery of brand-new Mills & Boon Enchanted novels, at least a month before they are available in the shops, FREE gifts and a monthly Newsletter packed with information, competitions, author profiles and lots more...

Accepting these FREE books and gift places you under no obligation to buy, you may cancel at any time, even after receiving just your free shipment. Simply complete the coupon below and send it to:

MILLS & BOON READER SERVICE, FREEPOST, CROYDON, SURREY, CR9 3WZ.

READERS IN EIRE PLEASE SEND COUPON TO PO BOX 4546, DUBLIN 24

NO STAMP NEEDED

Yes, please send me 4 free Enchanted novels and a mystery gift. I understand that unless you hear from me, I will receive 6 superb new titles every month for just £2.20* each, postage and packing free. I am under no obligation to purchase any books and I may cancel or suspend my subscription at any time, but the free books and gift will be mine to keep in any case. (I am over 18 years of age)

N7XE

Ms/Mrs/Miss/Mr_____
BLOCK CAPS PLEASE
Address_____

_____

_____ Postcode _____